D1293329

1

# The Bible

# Smuggler

## By LOUISE A. VERNON

Illustrated by ROGER HANE

HERALD PRESS, Scottdale, Pennsylvania/Kitchener, Ontario

# Contents

Chapter **1**

# *Death Before the Feast*

At noon Collin Hartley cast the last handful of
barley into the plowed ground, tossed the empty sack
over his shoulder, and started for the manor house a
mile away.

"Collin! Where do you think you're going?" Big
Jake, the overseer of the peasants, halted the oxen
near the road for the noonday rest.

Collin smiled. He was not afraid of Jake's bluff
ways. "Sir William° is going to take me up the hill
to the old Roman fort. He wants me to learn the
Latin names to things. After that I'm to be Lady
Walsh's page boy for the banquet tonight." Collin
unslung his sack. "See? I sowed all the barley seed."

Big Jake motioned for him to sit down, broke off
a hunk of brown bread, and handed a piece to
Collin. "So Sir William isn't satisfied teaching you
to read and write in English, eh?" He chuckled.
"He thinks you're a pretty smart boy, doesn't he?
But don't forget, *I* was the one who found you and
gave you a name. Ten years ago Easter, it was.
There you were, a newborn baby, abandoned in a

°In the sixteenth century, ordained preachers were called *Sir*, just like noblemen.

7

muddy ditch. You were no bigger than a handspan, but you yelled as loud as ten men."

Collin squirmed and nibbled his bread.

Jake chuckled again. "Does Lady Walsh know you're going with Sir William?"

His tone of voice troubled Collin. "Do you think she would mind?"

"I certainly do."

"But why?"

"Because you pester Sir William with questions all the time. After all, he is hired to tutor the Walsh children, not a peasant boy."

Collin felt his cheeks grow hot. "But I want to learn about things—about books. Words have magic. You've said so yourself, dozens of times."

Jake nodded. "Yes, words have magic—powerful magic. When Sir William preaches on Sabbath, his word-magic goes through my very bones. It's queer how such a little man can have so much power. What else can you call it but magic?"

Collin did not know how to answer. He finished his bread, picked up his sack, and grinned at Jake.

"When you get back from the fort," Jake said, "come and teach me what you learned, and I won't tell Lady Walsh where you were. Is that a bargain?"

Collin agreed, waved good-bye to Jake, and skipped along the road near the woods. A few minutes later the thud of hoofbeats startled him. Who could be coming to Little Sodbury in such a hurry this time of day? It couldn't be William Tyndale. He always walked to the village and back on the days he visited the sick.

A horseman holding a handkerchief to his face

galloped up and reined the horse to a stop. Blood streamed over the man's face from a cut on his forehead, but Collin could tell that the man was young.

"Don't you know me, Collin?" The cultured voice sounded urgent and somehow familiar.

Collin remembered. "Why, you're the messenger from Oxford University. What did you bring Sir William this time?"

"A most important book." The messenger tapped a bulky saddlebag. "A dangerous book." He twisted in the saddle and listened. "Did you see a band of monks come by here?"

"Why, no, sir. Why would they come to Little Sodbury?"

"Because they're after this book." Once again the messenger tapped the saddlebag. "They aren't really monks—they are Cardinal Wolsey's spies."

The word *spies* made Collin's scalp prickle. Cardinal Wolsey, the High Chancellor of England, had almost as much power as King Henry. But why would he send spies to a country manor house?

"Did they give you that cut over your eye?" he asked the messenger.

"No. A branch nicked me." The messenger looked at his bloodstained handkerchief. "But this is a sign of bloodshed to come."

Collin could not believe such words. Who would want to hurt anyone on such a beautiful spring day? Was the messenger from Oxford really telling the truth?

"I don't dare linger." The messenger scanned the woods with an uneasy glance. "These days anything

9

can happen." He leaned toward Collin. "God must have sent you to meet me. Are you a brave boy? Would you do something for Sir William?"

A feeling of daring loyalty quickened Collin's pulse. "I'll do anything for him. He's my teacher."

"See that he gets this book." The messenger lifted a heavy book from the saddlebag. "Don't let anyone see it."

Collin unslung his sack and laid the book inside. "What's the name of this book?"

"It's Luther's New Testament."

"Oh, I know about that," Collin said with satisfaction. "Sir William told me. Was it smuggled from Germany?"

The messenger nodded. "Yes, it was smuggled, and Cardinal Wolsey says that he will burn every copy he can find. His spies are everywhere, in all kinds of disguises; so be careful. Can you go to Sir William's room without being seen?"

Collin thought for a moment. "I'm sure I can get upstairs all right," he said. "Lady Walsh and the servants must be busy getting ready for the banquet tonight."

The messenger from Oxford turned his horse toward the woods. "If you think anyone is spying on you, hide the book." He added, "May God be with you."

When the messenger had gone, Collin started toward the manor house. With each step, Luther's New Testament grew heavier. Even a sackful of seed did not weigh as much. Collin hoisted the sack from one shoulder to the other. He kept close to the outbuildings, crossed the yard to the chapel, and then crept past the bushes bordering the large manor house.

The front entrance was empty. Collin tiptoed upstairs and set the sack on Tyndale's study table. He started to leave, then turned back. What word-magic had Luther put into his New Testament? Collin opened the book. To his disappointment he saw a mass of fat black letters with peaks and points. Collin could not make out one letter of the strange print. He sighed, wishing he knew as many languages as William Tyndale. Perhaps Sir William would let him learn German if he did well with Latin. Collin puzzled over the pages, forgetting the time.

Muffled shouts and high-pitched screams from downstairs sent the blood pounding through his body. He tiptoed to the top of the stairs and looked down into the entrance hall. Servants had just laid out a young man on the rushes near the door. Blood seeped through the young man's dark hair. Collin could not see his face, but he could tell it was the messenger from Oxford University, and he knew, too, that more than a tree branch had caused these wounds.

A strange fear swelled up within Collin. He clung to the banister watching the scene below.

Lady Walsh, holding her long skirts back, directed the servants to bring a basin of water and cloths. She turned from one servant to another. "Who is it? What was he doing here at Little Sodbury?"

No one could answer until Jake, looking out of place in his rough brown work tunic, pushed his way through the others. "I saw him staggering out of the woods, Lady Walsh. Three or four men with cowls over their heads kept hitting him with their staves. Whey they saw me, they ran back. That's all I can tell you."

11

A servant let out a piercing scream. "Lady Walsh! He's dead! He's dead!" She pointed to the limp figure. At once a groan of horror broke out from the others.

Lady Walsh turned white, put her hands to her throat, and closed her eyes for an instant. Then she straightened. "Nonsense. He's only fainted. Fix up a bed for him in the side room of the chapel. Tell no one about this. Remember, we have a banquet to-night. Important men of the church will be here in just a few more hours. Wash out the bloodstains and put clean rushes on the floor. All of you go back to your work."

When the entrance hall was empty, Collin started downstairs, sick and dizzy. Thoughts of the big book upstairs haunted him. That book, with its odd-shaped black letters, contained fatal word-magic. Death had come to the young man who carried the book. Collin knew without question that the messenger was dead. Lady Walsh's denial had not fooled him. If William Tyndale kept the book, would it not bring death to him also? Wouldn't it be better if Tyndale never saw the book?

Without hesitation, Collin ran back to William Tyndale's room and put Luther's New Testament into the sack. If he could manage to slip past the kitchen servants on the first floor, he would have no trouble reaching the stable. He could hide the book inside someplace.

The weight of the book, coupled with his growing fear, forced Collin to breathe in noisy gasps. At the bottom of the stairs he stopped to catch his breath. He could hear the servants talking.

"A bad omen—death before a banquet," a maid-servant said. "I feel so all-of-a-tremble, I don't know that I can keep on." Her voice rose. "Look at this mountain of vegetables. I thought men of the church didn't eat much."

Someone giggled. "They'll eat everything except the saltcellars." Her voice dropped into a hissing whisper. "To think there's a dead man out in the chapel. It gives me the shivers."

Collin heard the sound of iron kettles scraping the fireplace.

"Lady Walsh said he wasn't dead." he heard the cook say. "I've seen death before, and I know better. Why don't those church men get together and raise that poor young man to life? They keep coming here eating at Sir John's board and getting fatter all the time. What good is all their talk?"

"They come to hear William Tyndale, that's what. They say he knows almost more than anybody in England," another servant said. "I know for a fact, though, that a lot of those men are jealous of him."

Collin darted past the kitchen doorway. No one looked up. Without a backward glance, he raced toward the gloomy shadows of the stable doorway and stepped inside.

"Collin!" It was Lady Walsh's voice right behind him. "Come out and give me whatever it is you're hiding in that sack."

Trembling with the shock of discovery, Collin sprawled headlong into a feed bin. He let go of the sack and lay still, trying to shut out Lady Walsh's words.

"Come out, Collin." Lady Walsh spoke firmly.

13

Collin gritted his teeth, determined not to give up Luther's dangerous book. He turned to the stable doorway but did not look up at Lady Walsh. He knew exactly how she appeared—her brown eyes, straight nose, and small mouth; her hair hidden by the peaked headdress flowing to her shoulders. He caught a glimpse of the red embroidery of her gown —as red as the blood of the messenger. Luther's book would bring still more bloodshed. A book that brought death to people shouldn't be in anyone's hands.

"Give it to me, Collin, whatever it is you've taken from the house. What reason is there for you to steal? Haven't Sir John and I given you a home, clothes, and food? Don't you realize you are a waif, a foundling, an orphan?"

Collin bit his lip but said nothing.

"Answer me," Lady Walsh said. "I'm afraid you are a born troublemaker. What William Tyndale sees in you, I don't know."

A man's voice interrupted. "What is all this about, Lady Walsh?"

Collin looked up. William Tyndale, a small man with a long, narrow face and intense burning eyes, stood in the stable doorway. "They tell me a young man was brought here. Is that true? I have reason to believe he is a friend of mine from Oxford. Where is he?"

"In the chapel. Come with me." Lady Walsh turned away without another word to Collin.

With desperate speed, Collin burrowed into the deepest feed bin he could find and hid the sack containing Luther's New Testament. He waited until

14

almost dark before going back to the manor house. Lady Walsh was directing the servants with feverish intentness. When she saw Collin, she grasped him by the shoulder. He stiffened, expecting her to demand the book. Instead, she shook her head. "You can't serve my guests looking like that, Collin."

Collin looked down at his knee-length tunic. The coarse, unbleached cloth was stained from constant wear.

"My nephew wasn't much larger than you when he was my page boy. I wonder. . . . Wait here."

In a few moments she appeared with several garments over her arm and held them out to Collin. He fingered the silky cloth and as in a dream slipped on a finely woven white shirt with full sleeves tight at the wrists, a blue jerkin bound in velvet, and a flat circle of a cap of the same blue. He pulled up thigh-length hose and wriggled his feet into wide-toed leather shoes.

Lady Walsh murmured approvingly. "That's better. Now, go stand out front when the guests arrive, and direct the grooms to the stable. They can wait out there with the horses until the banquet is over."

Collin's heart lurched. There would be many horses, and the horses would nibble in the feed bins. What if they nuzzled Luther's book into the open? He knew it was not likely, and yet the thought bothered him so much he could not bear to think of leaving the book in the feed bin.

Already it was too late to go after it. The first guest had arrived on horseback. A groom on another horse rode behind. The guest, a fat, pasty-faced abbot, dismounted with many grunts and mutters. Collin disliked him at first sight. The abbot's wide-sleeved gown hung unevenly over his protruding stomach. A fringe of hair showed at the edge of his tight-fitting skull cap. Collin's distrust sprang from the peevish expression on the abbot's face and his biting comments to the groom, spoken so fast Collin could not hear. Perhaps this man was a spy for Cardinal Wolsey. Who could tell?

Collin directed the groom to the stable and then ran ahead to remove the sack containing Luther's book. With sudden inspiration, Collin packed feed around the book and fastened the top of the sack in a knot. But where could he hide it now?

The only thing to do was find William Tyndale and tell him the whole story. Collin started toward the house, then stopped. The abbot was talking in a surly voice. The groom kept nodding.

"Tyndale's no fool," the abbot said. "He knows exactly the trouble he's asking for by having Luther's heretical translation in his hands. Since you stupid fools lost track of the book this afternoon, we may expect it to turn up almost anyplace. Perhaps it's just as well. We can catch a lot of birds with one net later on."

Collin tried to scurry past unnoticed.

"Even this page boy here, with his heavy bundle, might be suspect," the abbot said in a heavy, jocular tone. Then he put his hand on Collin's shoulder. "Just a minute, boy. What do you have in that sack?"

Collin jerked free and ran toward the house.

"After him!" the abbot called to the groom. "See that he does not escape you."

*Collin runs to escape the abbot and his men.*

The heavy sack bobbed up and down on Collin's shoulders. He made a frantic effort to evade the groom's clutching hands, stumbled, and felt himself being dragged before the abbot. With a deep, shuddering breath, Collin let the sack fall to the ground.

## Chapter 2

## Secret Trial

The groom undid the knot and peered inside the sack. "Why, it's nothing but horse feed."

The abbot grunted and turned away without another word. When the grooms brought their horses to the stable, Collin shouldered his sack and slipped into the house. In Tyndale's room, out of breath, Collin could only point to the sack.

William Tyndale's face lit with understanding. "Luther's book?" he asked.

Collin nodded and shook the big book free of feed. Tyndale turned over the pages of Luther's New Testament with reverent care. A rustle of skirts sounded in the hall.

"Sir William, we are ready to eat. Please come down at once," Lady Walsh called.

Tyndale tucked Luther's New Testament under his arm and opened the door.

"Now, Sir William, I know the death of that young man is very distressing," Lady Walsh said, "but I have arranged for his body to be taken back to Oxford tonight. I beg you not to show grief before our guests. I for one can't believe Cardinal Wolsey is persecuting college students. At any rate, Sir John and I count on you to keep the dinner conversation brilliant, but don't let yourself be drawn into arguments, and above all, don't pound the table as I have seen you do on other occasions."

William Tyndale bowed. "You may rely on me to keep the conversation lively."

The grim, determined voice surprised Collin. He had never heard a tone like that from Tyndale before.

After Tyndale and Lady Walsh left, Collin hurried downstairs to his place in the dining hall. Sir John Walsh, the master of Little Sodbury, stood at the main table, his back to the fireplace, ready to welcome the guests. His dogs lay at his feet. When the guests streamed into the hall, the dogs set up a shrill chorus of barking. Sir John, ruddy-faced and beaming, did not seem to hear the dogs.

Collin had never seen so many high-ranking men at one time. All wore flowing robes with either tight-fitting caps or pancake-flat berets. Some of the men were lantern-jawed and stooped; some were skeleton thin, some plump and bulging. The glitter of their jeweled rings, chains, and crosses hurt Collin's eyes. The guests kept glancing at the well-filled table with its steaming food. When Sir John gave the signal to sit, Collin noticed that the guests lost no time in pulling back the benches and settling themselves for the feast.

Manor house servants scurried from kitchen to dining hall, laden with bulky pitchers and platters of food. Collin darted from place to place, helping to serve. The talk flowed on all sides. Collin hovered close to Tyndale's table.

"Sir William," a priest challenged, "you're stirring up much comment in these parts with your preaching on the Bristol green."

Collin sensed bitter unfriendliness in the man's voice.

William Tyndale's eyes flashed. "At least I'm not using the alehouse as my preaching place, like some barking curs I know of who are trying to discredit my name. I neither roar out with open and foaming mouth, nor mumble mass, matins, and evensong like a jaybird."

The priest choked on a bit of food and did not reply.

"Some say your views are a disturbance," another priest ventured.

Tyndale reached for his saltcellar and held it up. "The nature of salt is to bite, fret, and make smart, is it not? The office of a true preacher is to salt. And," he added, "true preaching stirs up persecution."

"But do you not fear a charge of heresy?" another guest asked.

William Tyndale snorted. "Heresy? The source of all heresies is pride. I have said nothing that cannot be justified out of the New Testament."

Collin listened, shifting from one foot to the other. An undercurrent of antagonism, even hatred, lay below the surface of the well-mannered guests. He hoped William Tyndale would not argue, even in good humor. But Collin saw that Tyndale was just warming up.

"There are twenty thousand priests in England today who mumble from morning to night, not knowing what they say. They can't even translate '*Fiat voluntas tua sicut in coelo et in terra.*' " (Thy will be done on earth as it is in heaven.)

"Why should they translate it?" the abbot, leaning forward, asked with a sneer. "Latin is the language of the church."

"Jesus didn't know Latin." Tyndale slapped the table with his open hand. "Why should English curates sing and say and patter Latin with the lips only? Their hearts understand nothing, but Scripture says God is love and will be served with love."

Someone interrupted in a loud voice. "Are we to be tutored by a boy just out of college?"

Voices buzzed. The abbot leaned forward again, waving his knife. "Is it not true that you have a heretical book in your possession?"

Collin gasped. Did the abbot really know—or was he just making a guess?

William Tyndale put his hand on the book by his plate. "Why, no. I do not have a heretical book. I do, however, have a copy of Martin Luther's New Testament."

The flat statement had a curious numbing effect on all within earshot. A sudden, frightening silence fell. The guests, with averted eyes, whispered to one another. Fat lips, thin lips, buttoned-up lips—all shaped the words, "Luther's New Testament."

Everyone stared at William Tyndale. Collin saw no smiles on faces suddenly turned white, only lines of fear. He marveled at the magic of words. Why would the words "Luther's New Testament" frighten a roomful of important men?

22

The whispered message reached Sir John, who stood up and rapped for attention. "What is this about Luther's New Testament?"

The abbot stood up. His wide sleeves fell back from his arm as he pointed a fat forefinger at William Tyndale. "This—this *heretic*—" The abbot sputtered and gasped for breath. His face grew mottled and puffy with anger. He made another attempt to speak. "This traitor to God has in his hands the German heretic's book." The abbot swayed forward, bracing himself with both hands on the table. "Why, I keep Martin Luther's portrait by my desk—"

An exclamation of horror burst from every throat.

"—so I can *spit* on it." The abbot wiped his mouth with his hand. "And you admit you have in your possession a work by this infidel, this heretic?"

Collin cringed at the triumph in the abbot's voice, and thought of the young messenger from Oxford, lying dead. A more terrifying image rose in his mind. What if there were another ambush—this time with William Tyndale as the victim? Cold sweat broke out in Collin's hands.

Tyndale rose and faced the abbot. Silence enveloped the room. Only the fire sputtered, as if in agreement with the abbot's accusation.

"Martin Luther is not a heretic," Tyndale said. "He does not have the pride which is the source of all true heresies. The Word of God strips man of everything and leaves him as bare as Job, and this Luther has, this oneness with God from the Word of God. He has translated God's own Word into the language of the people."

The abbot made a sharp retort. "Have you for-

23

gotten that two years ago—in 1521—our cardinal required all such literature to be surrendered to him?"

Tyndale grimaced. "Cardinal Wolsey—Wolfsee, the wily wolf?"

No one laughed at the daring joke. An involuntary shudder passed through Collin. How did William Tyndale dare make light of such a serious matter?

Sir John rapped on the table again. "Let me see this book."

At a signal from Tyndale, Collin carried the book to Sir John's table.

"Why, this is in German." Sir John looked dismayed. "Sir William, you'll have to translate this for us."

For a moment the church men quieted under Sir John's approval; then like a winter storm an ominous undertone gathered force.

An old man stood up at his place and with a trembling finger pointed toward the fireplace. "Sir William, please throw this horrible book into the fire. Let it burn instead of you, for as sure as God witnesses within me, that will be your fate in the future if you do not stop your heretical preaching."

As if at a signal, a log crashed in the fireplace sending up a shower of sparks.

In the uneasy quiet, Tyndale leaped up on his bench to address the whole hall. Even standing, he looked small and defenseless. A fierce burning and longing surged through Collin. He longed to protect his teacher, fight for him, pledge his life to serve him.

"You would burn those who, like Luther, teach Christ's truth," Tyndale was saying. "If you could,

24

you would burn the Scriptures themselves."

With loud outcries, the church men scrambled to their feet.

"Shall we knowingly consort with a heretic?" the abbot cried out. "This man will be the death of us all."

The guests stampeded toward the door, knocking over benches in their haste. The dogs howled in a frenzy of excitement. Sir John tried to calm his guests, but no one listened. Lady Walsh watched from the doorway, her face white and strained. Collin began to right the overturned benches.

The clamor must have reached outside. Jake, the overseer, appeared and, with a wary glance toward the entrance hall, tiptoed up to Collin.

"What happened in here?"

Collin poured out every detail.

Jake rubbed his ear. "But Sir William is a fine man. Why, he prayed over my wife when she was deathly sick, and she's well now. Then there's old daft Darty. Sir William talked to him with his word-magic book, and old Darty is as good a man in the field as any I have. Sir William is a real Christian. Why would anyone be upset by what he said?"

Collin could not explain why, though he knew now that word-magic could work two ways, and he knew, too, that he wanted to stay close to William Tyndale.

¤   ¤   ¤

To Collin's joy, Lady Walsh later ordered him to remain in the manor house as her page boy. A few days after the ill-fated banquet, a drizzling rain chilled the whole house. Lady Walsh ordered the fire lit in the dining hall. William Tyndale brought the Walsh children downstairs for their game period. From the kitchen, Collin heard the children laugh and tiptoed to watch. The cheerful crackling of the logs and the children's chatter helped Collin forget the nightmare banquet of a few days before.

"Let's play hot cockles, Sir William." Maurice the six-year-old, held out a blindfold.

The smaller children clapped their hands. "Yes, yes."

Maurice tied the blindfold around William Tyndale's eyes. "Turn him around."

With much giggling, the children turned Tyndale around and around until he staggered from loss of balance.

"Put your hands behind your back." Maurice pulled Tyndale's hands into place. "Now, one of us will hit your hands, and you have to guess who. If you can't guess, you'll have to stay *it*."

The children, each in turn, hit his hands. Tyndale could not guess the right one. Each time, he let himself be whirled around. Then Maurice looked at Collin.

"You hit his hands," he whispered. "He'll never guess."

In his eagerness to join the game, Collin tripped on a toy stick horse lying on the floor. He stumbled, knocking Tyndale toward the fireplace.

"Look out for the fire, Sir William," Collin called, but he was too late. Tyndale fell on the burning log. Sparks, flames, and ashes rose about him. The children screamed. Collin caught Tyndale's flailing hand and tugged with every ounce of strength he had. Tyndale sprawled sideways out of the fire. Collin, with bare hands, brushed off the sparks on Tyndale's robe.

Tyndale lay without moving, still blindfolded. His close-fitting black velvet cap had fallen off. His beard was singed. He struggled to a sitting position, head up, as if someone had called him.

"Blindfolded," he whispered in such a deep, strange voice that the children huddled wordless, staring at him.

"Men, women, and children—blindfolded—groping for God's truth. The church must bring Christ to its people, and in their own tongue." Tyndale trembled and gripped his hands together. "And I—I am chosen to take the blindfold off people's eyes. I?" he questioned in an agonized voice, struggling to his knees. "God, are you sure you want *me*?"

Collin felt such a sense of *Presence* in the room that he, too, dropped to his knees. The Walsh children, still wordless, did the same. There was not a whimper or a stir from even the smallest child.

Then, like a soundless wind, the *Presence* whirled away. Tyndale tore off the bandage and put his hand across his eyes. Maurice ran for his mother, who hurried in and alternately sympathized and scolded William Tyndale.

"Do be careful, Sir William," she said. "But if you are sure you are all right, there is a messenger from the chancellor to see you. Collin, go bring him in here."

The messenger came to the point at once. "You are wanted for questioning at the village."

Lady Walsh looked frightened. "Questioning? What for?"

The messenger did not answer her. "For private questioning," he told Tyndale.

There was a moment's silence.

"You mean a secret trial, do you not?" Tyndale asked in a gentle voice. "Though I think there was a secret trial the other night."

"It's the priests," the messenger said. "They say you're going to translate the Bible into English and they have sworn to stop it."

Tyndale's mouth dropped open in surprise. "But how could they know? I just got the message myself a minute ago."

"What message?" Lady Walsh's voice was sharp.

"Why, that I'm to translate the Bible into English."

With a look of horror, Lady Walsh tugged at Tyndale's sleeve. "You can't do that. Nobody can. Have you lost your senses completely? The church will never rest until it burns you at the stake. How can you have such a wicked, foolish idea?" Without warning her face softened. "No, it is the church that is wicked, and the cardinal, who represents the church. You *must* translate the Bible into English, Sir William, and may God be with you every step of the way."

Tyndale seemed to understand the change in Lady Walsh. His smile was tender. "What mortal can withstand His power?" He turned to the messenger. "I am ready to go."

As soon as they left, Lady Walsh turned to Collin. "Follow Sir William. Don't let him see you. If anything unusual happens, run back and tell us at once."

Collin nodded, filled with both a rising excitement and a nameless fear. He hurried outside. The rain had stopped. He sniffed the good clean smell rising from the wet trees and shrubs. Confused thoughts tumbled about in his mind. Above all, one idea was strong. There was a magic stronger than the word-magic, and that was the power of God. But what happened when men misunderstood God's power? Collin quickened his steps. He must not let Tyndale out of his sight.

Some distance ahead, men's voices rose in the quiet air. Collin watched a group of monks and priests, each armed with a thick staff, approach Tyndale.

"This is the heretic," one called out. He lifted his arm to strike.

A crushing, blinding terror paralyzed Collin. He turned to run back to the manor house, but a thick hand clamped over his mouth. He felt his arms pinioned behind him. Someone pulled him backward into a clump of bushes.

## Chapter 3

# No Room for Heretics

Collin twisted and kicked, but the man's powerful grip did not loosen. In exhaustion and utter helplessness, Collin went limp. At once the man released him.

"Easy, lad. Don't make any noise. I don't want them to know we're here." Jake's voice rumbled in Collin's ear. "Mind, not a sound."

Collin nodded, rubbing his arms.

"My men are right behind me." Jake nodded over his shoulder. "We've known for a long time that the priests have been talking against Sir William. We've all heard them one time or another at the village. You can take my word for it, we're not going to let anything happen to Sir William." Jake parted the shrubbery and peered out.

Collin stood on tiptoe behind him and looked, too. William Tyndale was facing the monks and priests, many of them with upraised staffs, yet no one seemed ready to hit Tyndale.

"What is it you want?" Tyndale asked the group.

A monk muffled in brown robe and cowl stepped forward. His cowl slipped off, revealing the man's full face. He had the reddest beard Collin had ever seen. His hair was a darker red. Collin heard Tyndale gasp.

"John—John Tisen," he said. "What are you doing this far from Oxford?"

John Tisen's small, wide-set eyes narrowed. "I'm not your scholar anymore, Sir William. I have done much penance for the untruths you taught."

Collin jerked in silent protest. At once Jake's hand clamped on his shoulder in warning. Collin watched the scene taking place in front of him.

"So you became a monk?" William Tyndale asked his former pupil. The red-bearded man shrugged. "I am in Cardinal Wolsey's service." He smiled in a one-sided, sly way.

"You mean you are a spy?" William Tyndale's voice deepened in contempt, and John Tisen flinched. Collin could see a spasm cross his face.

"Sir William, why do you go against the church's policy?" John Tisen asked. "The path you are following leads to sure destruction. I warn you that I have taken my stand against heretics."

For some reason, these words caused many of the group to relax and lower their staffs. Collin caught sight of a movement in a nearby field. A young boy had stopped his oxen and was picking his way over the fresh furrows toward the road. Collin could see both fear and curiosity in the boy's face.

William Tyndale glanced at the boy and then back to the group. "The path I am following, John, means that if God spares my life, before many years, I will cause a boy who drives a plow to know more of the Scripture than you do."

31

At these words, the monks and priests set up such a shout that the plowboy ran back to his oxen. Jake motioned his men to come closer.

"Take him to Chancellor Parker," a priest shouted. The group closed in around Tyndale and half pushed and half carried him toward the village.

"What will you do now?" Collin implored Jake.

"We'll go the other way around to the village and hide outside the meeting place. The villagers will help us. We'll fight if we have to."

"Lady Walsh told me to keep Sir William in sight," Collin said.

"Then you follow them, and mind that you don't show yourself." Jake led his men in another direction.

At the village, Collin saw the group take William Tyndale to a small meeting room. There was no guard at the door, and Collin slipped behind a wooden column to listen. His heart beat so loud he was afraid someone would hear, but all the men were talking at once.

"What have we here?" the chancellor roared.

"Chancellor Parker, this is William Tyndale, who preaches against the faith," John Tisen replied.

In a voice of authority, William Tyndale asked, "What is it you have against me?"

"This man is a heretic," John Tisen said.

"And where are your witnesses to my heresy?" William Tyndale asked. "Let them come forward and I will answer them."

From the rustle and scraping of feet, Collin expected several to witness against Tyndale, but the movements subsided into nervous coughs and clearing of throats.

*William Tyndale answers Chancellor Parker.*

The chancellor himself began to accuse Tyndale. "I have heard about you. I understand you called monks and friars of the church *caterpillars, horse-leeches,* and *drone bees.*"

"You make a little gnat into a great elephant," Tyndale replied. "Is this all you accuse me of?"

"How is it that you dare speak of translating the Bible into English?"

Collin clung to the column. A sudden, overpowering heat filled the room. It was as if hate and fear rolled out in waves. Then he became aware of William Tyndale's cool, quiet strength. It flashed into Collin's mind that Tyndale was praying, and it seemed to Collin that God was filling Tyndale with His power.

"The Gospel must speak to us in the language of our own people," Tyndale urged. "Christians must read the Bible in their mother tongue."

Hisses and growls rose from the group. Collin peered out. All he could see was a mass of upraised, clenched fists, and he quickly drew back. He was helpless. Then he realized he was supposed to go back to the manor house, but it was too late now.

Chancellor Parker quieted the group. "The truth is before the people in the way God meant it," he snapped to Tyndale. "He gives it personally to the ordained."

"God did not tell those who perform divine service in Latin to be ignorant of what they read," Tyndale replied, calm and decisive.

"You think you can say these things because you're protected by a rich man," the chancellor said. "You'll find out otherwise."

34

A priest spoke out. "Do not bring Sir. John's name into this. He is a powerful gentleman in this country."

The chancellor grunted. "I say to you, Sir William, that it's the favor of the gentry of the country that makes you so proud. But you shall not always live in a fine manor house."

"I have never preached anything that cannot be justified from the New Testament," Tyndale said. "But I ask, Has not God made the English tongue as well as Latin?"

The uproar this time was tremendous. Collin looked out in time to see John Tisen swing his staff over his head. "Shall we listen any longer? Shall this man pollute and poison innocent people's minds?"

The others howled a response. "No—no." They lunged toward Tyndale with arms upraised. Collin shouted a warning. Jake and eight or ten sturdy peasants armed with mallets and stones swarmed into the room.

"Stop!" The chancellor's command was more a pathetic screech than an order. "The church will excommunicate all of you."

Jake planted his feet apart and waved his mallet. "We have no quarrel with the church, no quarrel at all, but we want our Sir William to stay right here. Isn't that so?"

The peasants shouted a ringing "yes," echoed by villagers coming in the door.

"That may be," the chancellor said, "but it is against the law for anyone to translate the Bible into English. That is heresy, and if this man is guilty, he will answer for it."

"But he hasn't done it yet, and the law holds no man accountable for what he hasn't done." Jake's angry voice filled the little building.

There were mutters of assent. John Tisen gripped his staff. "We will run him out of the country if he ever starts. We will see that he has no place to turn to for help. We'll pursue him to the ends of the earth if necessary. Cardinal Wolsey will see to it."

Tyndale mounted a bench and spread his hands over the group. "Take away my goods, take away my good name, yet so long as Christ dwells in my heart, so long shall I love you not a whit less for these words."

Jake and his men made no move to go. With much grumbling and venomous undertones, the priests left. Collin ran up to Tyndale. "What will they do now?" he asked.

Jake thumped his mallet on the floor. "We'll keep you here safely. You're needed to help our sick and poor."

Tyndale smiled. "The church may send me where it will. If I have ten pounds a year to live on and am bound to nothing but to teach children, preach, and fulfill my mission, I will be content anyplace in England."

Dogs barked outside. Sir John, flushed and disheveled, strode in. He ordered Jake and the peasants to go back to the fields at Little Sodbury. Then he turned to Tyndale. "Sir William, unless you muzzle yourself, there're certain to be other attacks on you. Your friends won't be able to save you every time. Now, tell me what happened."

Outside, Sir John motioned to Collin to lead the

36

horse. The two men walked ahead. Collin could see that Sir John was upset. He swung his riding whip back and forth, flicking a dog that came too close, or nipping off the top of a plant.

"Chancellor Parker was not civil to me," Tyndale said, "but he did not change my purpose. Christians must possess the holy Scriptures in their own tongue. Without direct knowledge of the Bible, ordinary people can never know God's truth."

Sir John swished his whip through the air. "But *heresy—*"

"Is it heretical to question why people must pray in a language they don't understand? Are we to teach our children this way? Look at Collin here. He's ten. He should be able to read the Scriptures by himself. Maurice is six. Do you want your own son to grow up in ignorance of God's truth?"

Sir John stopped. "Of course I want my sons to be educated, but I must say I can't see my peasants quoting Scripture. Why, first thing you know, they'll all be wanting to go to Oxford for an education. But you can stay at Little Sodbury as long as you wish. Just try to keep quiet about your translating, will you?"

William Tyndale put his hands behind his back and walked to one side of the road. Collin, puzzled, watched him. Sir John stood silent.

As if he had come to a decision, Tyndale turned. "Sir John, I perceive that I shall not be allowed to tarry long here, nor shall you be able to keep me out of the hands of the priests. I should be right sorry if anything unpleasant should occur."

Collin was troubled by the words. What was

Tyndale really saying?

"If you insist on translating the Bible into English, there's no question but that the priests will hound you."

Tyndale looked up at Sir John. "God knows what troubles you would expose yourself to by keeping me in your family. Permit me to leave you."

The words struck Collin like a blow. He stared at the ground in misery. Would Tyndale really leave Little Sodbury and go to some unknown place where Collin would never see him again?

Sir John made a quick protest. "How do you know that to go away isn't cowardly? Does God want you to flee before men?"

"I am now the instrument of God," Tyndale said. "He knows the ways of men. Call it cowardice or what you will, I must accomplish my task by the means at hand, even by another name, or in disguise, if I must."

As Collin listened, his desire to go with Tyndale, to be with him and help him, grew so strong he could hardly keep quiet. Sir John mounted his horse.

"I'll go ahead and tell Lady Walsh about this," he said, then added, "Wouldn't someone at Cambridge help you get another preaching post?"

"I know Fisher," Tyndale said, "but he's not in good repute with the church at present."

"How about Langland at Oxford?"

Tyndale shrugged. "Useless. His episcopal career is already well established. He wouldn't take the risk with me. I don't know anyone I could count on. One of my own students led the group today. He's in Cardinal Wolsey's pay."

Collin remembered the man with the red beard—John Tisen, and marveled that anyone who had been taught by William Tyndale could turn against him.

Sir John dismounted. "If you wanted to go to London, I could write a letter of introduction to Sir Henry Guildford, the king's controller of the household."

William Tyndale brightened. "If I could be appointed chaplain in London—yes, that would be ideal."

"You must go to Cuthbert Tonstall, the Bishop of London." Sir John sounded really excited. "He's the one who can help you."

The two men talked on. Collin, head drooping, felt lonelier than he ever had in his life.

"But tone it down, Tyndale," Sir John was saying. "Try not to stir the people too much."

William Tyndale laughed an open hearty laugh. For the first time that day, Collin felt the weight of dread lift from his own heart.

Lady Walsh pounced on him and drew him to one side. "You were supposed to come back and report. If Sir John had known what Jake was up to, he could have prevented such a disgraceful display. We cannot afford to make the church and the cardinal our enemy, no matter how brilliant Sir William is. Now, Collin, your first loyalty was to us. I'm sorry you saw fit to think otherwise. I'm sending you back to the fields. I don't want to see you around the house again."

Heartsick and dismayed, Collin could only stare at Lady Walsh. Her face stern, she pointed toward the fields. There was nothing for Collin to do but obey. He fought back his tears and stumbled away.

## Chapter 4

## Unwilling Witness

Collin found Jake and told him the story. Jake was sympathetic. "Lady Walsh is a good woman," he said, "but changeable. First thing you know, she'll want you back, and I must say you belong to the manor house. You're too little to be a good field hand, though you're quick to learn. Why don't you go talk to Sir William? He'll know what's best."

Jake's hint was enough. Collin hurried to William Tyndale's room. The door was half open, and Collin could see Tyndale sitting at his study table. Three books lay propped open near his hand. Tyndale looked at a sheaf of papers and nibbled at the end of a quill pen. He shook his head and muttered something. Then he studied the books, wrote a few words, read them aloud, shook his head, and scratched out what he had written.

Collin did not dare interrupt him. He watched Tyndale for a long time. It began to occur to Collin that William Tyndale was not going to stop his work for meals. Collin's own hunger pangs drove him to the kitchen. The cook fed him and prepared a tray of food for Tyndale. Collin brought the food to

40

Tyndale's room, but Tyndale still did not look up. Humming and waving his hand in a regular beat, Tyndale chanted words. He had the look of a man gazing at mountaintops.

"He has to eat sometime," Collin told himself. He tore off a bit of bread and put it within range of Tyndale's fingers. To Collin's gratification, Tyndale's fingers, as if they were not part of his conscious self, closed around the bread, and the next minute, he had plopped it into his mouth. Collin fed Tyndale the whole meal bite by bite.

With a start, Tyndale focused his eyes on Collin. "Oh, I didn't know you were here. Good. Listen to this, and tell me if you understand what I'm saying." He read a long sentence in English. "Do you know what that means?"

"No, sir, not exactly." Collin had not understood a word.

Tyndale sighed. "I was afraid of that. I have put words clean contrary to the meaning of the Scripture, yet I know there is but one simple, literal sense. How did Luther ever manage the German language?"

A knock at the door interrupted him. Lady Walsh hurried in. "Sir William, there is another summons for you. Perhaps it would be best if you left early tomorrow. We'll have two saddle horses for you and your books." Her gaze fell on Collin. "Why, Collin Hartley, what are you doing here? Still the troublemaker, eh? Well, after Sir William leaves, I'll attend to you."

Collin waited until Lady Walsh left and eased himself out of the room. He ran to the stable and crouched in a dark corner. It was plain that he was of no use to anyone. Hugging his knees, Collin brooded for a long time. There must be something worthwhile he could do. If only he would get a message from God, like William Tyndale's. Collin looked up hopefully, remembering how Tyndale had looked when he received the inspiration to translate the Bible. But nothing happened to Collin either inwardly or from the outside.

He brooded again. He had liked working in the manor house. Perhaps there were other manor houses in England where he could work. He still wore his page boy clothes. In a flash, he knew what he was going to do. He would run away. That must be God's message to him.

Exhausted, Collin curled up and went to sleep, waking when someone shook him by the shoulder. He looked up into Jake's homely, concerned face.

"Collin! What are you doing here? Sir William is leaving. Lady Walsh has been looking for you."

Collin's pulse thudded. Jerking free, he dashed for the doorway and ran right into Sir John, Lady Walsh, and William Tyndale. Sir John's dogs barked and leaped toward Collin. Sir John quieted them with a thick walking stick. Collin felt a new fear. Was Sir John going to beat him in front of William Tyndale? More than ever, Collin determined to run away, but still, he *had* disobeyed Lady Walsh. He would have to put things right before he left.

"I'm sorry I went into the house again, Lady Walsh. I asked the cook for something to eat and then I took a tray to Sir William, because he forgot to eat, and—"

To his surprise, Lady Walsh laughed. Sir John

spoke in good humor. "That settles it. Take the boy with you, by all means, Sir William. I can see he'll take good care of you."

In dazed hope, Collin could only stare at Sir John.

"I wash my hands of you, Collin," Lady Walsh said, but she did not sound cross.

"Perhaps he doesn't want to go with me," Tyndale suggested.

"*Do* I?" The words came out in such a yelp of excitement that Sir John's dogs started to bark.

Jake brought up two horses and tightened the pack saddles on each side. "Take good care of Sir William," he whispered. "He's a man of God."

A few moments later, Collin and William Tyndale mounted the horses. Collin turned for a last look at Little Sodbury. Its sharply angled gables, gray roofs, and gray walls stood stark against the sky as if it had been forced out of the rocky ground.

Tyndale stared out over the valley and then turned to Collin. "We have many days of travel ahead. Since we didn't get up to the old Roman fort for your Latin lesson, we can start now."

In the next few days of travel, Collin learned many Latin words. One day at the noon rest, Collin remembered his impulse to run away.

"Would God ever tell a person to do something wrong?" he blurted.

"No, Collin. God does not tell you to do something wrong, but sometimes man misunderstands His message."

Collin felt better, but he was not quite satisfied. "Then how can you tell it's God giving the message?"

Collin hesitated, then told Tyndale of his impulse. "Wasn't God telling me to run away?"

Tyndale answered with a question of his own. "Did you feel good about running away?"

"No." Collin reflected for a moment. "You mean if God is with you, you feel good even if you have troubles?"

Tyndale smiled agreement and gave the signal to mount the horses. Collin smiled, too, ready to tackle the afternoon's Latin lesson.

o   o   o

The day came when William Tyndale pointed out a ring of walls several miles ahead. "There's London."

Beyond the city gates Collin could see gardens, fields, and moors rimmed with wooded slopes and thick woods. Once through the city gates city life burst all around Collin. The noises, sights, and smells made him dizzy. Thick timbered buildings hunched over him. The narrow streets were filled with people jostling each other as they came and went. On all sides, Collin heard sounds, some harsh, some pleasant. Carpenters sawed lumber. Weavers' shuttles clicked and clacked. Blacksmiths' anvils rang. Coppersmiths pounded kettles into shape.

But it was the smell of London that bothered Collin most. No matter how he twisted, turned, or stood tall, he could not rid his nostrils of the smell of rotting vegetables and other refuse. Then he sniffed a savory smell coming from a tiny shop opening on the sidewalk. A cook at a booth called out,

"Hot pies, hot pies!" Collin stood so long watching that Tyndale laughed and bought each of them a pie.

Later, Tyndale entered a snug little inn while Collin stood outside with the horses. The landlord bustled out, and after a searching glance at Collin's and Tyndale's dusty clothes and travel-weary horses, refused to handle the money Tyndale held out. Instead, he motioned Collin and Tyndale inside, pointed to a pot of vinegar, and signaled Tyndale to drop the money in it.

"Prevents plague," the landlord said. "We haven't had it lately, but a body never knows what travelers will bring with them."

The landlord's haughty air made Collin uncomfortable. Then William Tyndale took out his letters of introduction with their magnificent waxed seals. The landlord's eyes widened.

"I'm going to preach here in London. I don't know just where yet," Tyndale said. When he asked where the Bishop of London's palace was, the landlord beamed, bowed, and rubbed his hands. It amused Collin a few days later to see the pride on the landlord's face when the rector of St.-Dunstan-in-the-West called in person to ask Tyndale to preach in his church.

"Go hear Sir William Tyndale," the landlord urged his guests weeks later. "Marvelous preacher. Congregation has doubled since he came to London."

Collin could tell that Tyndale was pleased to be able to preach to so many people. Every day he worked on his translation of the Bible, and every day he helped Collin with Latin and English lessons.

Every day, too, he had been going to the Bishop of London's palace, near St. Paul's Cathedral, with his letters of introduction.

"I don't understand it," Tyndale said one day, pacing the little inn parlor. "My petition is always refused. Why?"

Collin determined to find out. The next day he rose early and completed his study lesson for the day. That afternoon he followed Tyndale to the bishop's palace. A stream of petitioners filed into the antechamber. Some were so old and bent they stumbled on their long robes. Others, young and dressed in bright colors, pranced about, twitching their capes over their shoulders and chattering with one another. An assistant in livery came into the room. "The bishop has had to leave for an important meeting at St. Paul's. Come back tomorrow," he said.

There was a moan of disappointment among the petitioners. Collin hurried out before Tyndale could have a chance to see him. Outside in the courtyard, a richly dressed portly man mounted a horse covered with gold spangles. It could only be the bishop himself. Collin wove his way through the crowd and followed the bishop, who was accompanied by a group of men on horseback.

In the streets people bowed and made way for the procession. At St. Paul's Cathedral, the men dismounted and went inside. The nave of the church was thronged with pilgrims buying souvenirs at little stalls tucked between stone niches, and Collin soon lost sight of the bishop and his party. Fascinated, Collin watched the crowd buying, selling, and talking.

He wandered about until a shrill whistle caught

his attention. It seemed to come from his feet. He looked down. A boy about his own age, with tangled dark hair and dark, intense eyes, squatted under the arch of a stone column. The boy grinned in such an easy, impudent, knowing, and friendly way that Collin grinned back.

The boy beckoned and said something Collin could not understand. "I've been watching you," the boy said in English. "You're new here."

"How can you tell?" Collin was genuinely astonished, for in his page's dress, he felt quite in keeping with the native Londoners in their bright clothes.

The boy tapped the pavement with a hooked stick. "I can tell by the way you gawk at things." He craned his neck back, widened his eyes, and let his mouth drop open in such a foolish imitation that Collin laughed in spite of himself.

"What language were you speaking at first?"

"Oh, that's German. My mother is German," the boy said shortly. His eyes never ceased a restless scanning of the crowd. A young man tossed an apple core away. The boy pounced on it, took one bite, and put the rest of the core in a little sack at his waist, tucking it and a black velvet purse out of sight.

*He's hungry*, Collin thought, *but why didn't he eat it all?*

The boy wiggled his stick, snagged a white lace handkerchief from a young dandy's sleeve, and tucked it into his ragged shirt. Collin noticed that the boy's waist bulged. The boy must be a thief.

"Bet you couldn't do that in a hundred years," the boy laughed.

47

"Buy why did you do it? That's stealing," Collin said.

"What do you mean, stealing? Someone's old apple core? I'm hungry, and he didn't want it." A look of brooding sadness crossed the boy's face.

"No, not the apple core," Collin said. "The fine lace handkerchief and that velvet purse I saw you hide. Wouldn't you be punished if you got caught?"

"Beaten within an inch of my life." The boy sounded cheerful now. "Those fools—they deserve to lose their fine laces and their purses, too. They don't have to worry about what they're going to eat." A peculiar, hardened bitterness crept into his voice. Then he grinned again. "I'll teach you how, if you like. It's quite an art, but you look quick."

"Thank you, but I couldn't," Collin said. "It's against the commandments."

"Against what?" The other boy stared at Collin. "Why don't you stay with me and post yourself across the way? I'll teach you how to speak German and no one will understand us. I can give you signals that way. Between us, we could clean out fifty people a day."

Collin, shocked, yet intrigued, did not know what to say.

"What's your name?" he asked.

"What would you think?"

Taken aback, Collin could only stare. "How could I possibly know?"

"Well, where are we?"

"St. Paul's Cathedral."

"Then what's my name?"

"St. Paul."

The boy rocked with laughter. "No, I'm no saint. Saints look like this." He folded his hands on his chest and rolled his eyes back until the whites showed.

"Then your name must be just Paul."

"That's right. What's yours?"

"Collin Hartley."

A commotion stirred through the crowd swirling past. A woman with a sharp nose pointed toward Paul. "There he is, constable, that little boy over there."

Paul jumped up. A crafty, hunted expression crossed his face. He tossed the velvet purse to Collin. "Here, take this. Run the other way." Paul disappeared in the crowd. Collin saw the constable approach.

The woman flung herself toward Collin. "This boy must be an accomplice. Look! He's holding my purse." She grabbed the bag. "Cane him right here. That'll teach him to steal."

Before he quite knew what was happening, Collin felt a thwack across his shoulders. The constable laid on the blows thick and fast, pausing only because a procession was coming out of the cathedral. Collin glimpsed the Bishop of London himself looking at the scene with an amused smile.

"Whose page boy is this?" the bishop asked.

"Your reverence," the sharp-nosed woman said, "this boy was caught stealing my purse."

"Yes, yes, and now you have it back. Whose page is he?"

Collin's mind whirled. He did not dare mention William Tyndale's name. The bishop would never listen to a man whose page boy had disgraced him in public.

Collin hung his head and said nothing.

The bishop moved on. "Find out, John," he told an assistant.

Collin looked up. A red-bearded young man stared at him first in puzzlement, then with growing recognition. The bishop's assistant was John Tisen, William Tyndale's former student, the spy of Cardinal Wolsey.

Far from being a help to William Tyndale, Collin had now only made things worse.

## Chapter 5

## *Invitation to Leave*

The constable turned to the red-bearded man. "Aren't you John Tisen, the bishop's assistant?"

Tisen nodded and frowned at Collin. "I seem to remember this young thief. Where is his master?"

A new voice broke in. "I'm his master." William Tyndale pushed his way through the crowd to Collin's side.

"Ah, yes, Sir William." John Tisen smiled and bowed. "I think heretics and thieves go well together."

The venom in John Tisen's voice made chills go down Collin's spine.

William Tyndale put both hands on Collin's shoulders and faced John Tisen. "What is this all about? Collin is a good Christian boy, and I will be responsible for his actions."

Collin squirmed with the mixed feelings of gratitude and humiliation. His breath quickened. He could not tell on Paul, because Paul needed help. There was a mystery about his new friend, and Collin meant to find out more.

"I'm willing to take the punishment," Collin said,

bracing himself for more blows. "I—I want to," he told William Tyndale.

The crowd murmured in protest. "No, no. That's enough. He's learned his lesson."

The woman with the purse stepped forward. "Yes, it's quite enough." John Tisen glanced over the crowd and shrugged. "I'm sure if the matter hasn't been taken care of properly, it will be."

The threatening undercurrent of his words troubled Collin. As Cardinal Wolsey's spy, John Tisen had threatened to pursue William Tyndale to the ends of the earth in order to prevent the translation of the Bible. The Bishop of London would undoubtedly agree with the cardinal. Collin tried to put the troublesome thoughts out of his mind.

The next day he came back to the cathedral. Paul sat on his heels in the same place under the stone arch.

"I hear you took a beating for me yesterday— and you didn't tell on me. Thanks. You're all right."

Astonished, Collin asked, "But how did you find that out?"

Paul threw back his head and laughed. "It's plain you weren't born in London. You've got a lot to learn if you stay here. Watch this." Putting his two fingers in his mouth, Paul whistled an odd little sound. Immediately the same whistle was echoed from a beggar near the entrance, then from an apple woman, a souvenir salesman, and a man holding horses.

"What does it all mean?" Collin asked.

Paul looked smug. "The people I know all help each other, and me especially. It's really because of my father. He died saving a lot of people."

Paul did not continue, but pointed out all his friends. "They wouldn't have let you be really hurt yesterday. They were all watching. I've got to get to work now."

Collin soon saw that Paul worked hard running errands for rich people, often carrying important purchases for them.

"Why don't you steal those things?" Collin asked.

Paul was scornful. "Because they trust me. People I know are particular about what they steal. It's only the people who put on airs that we fleece."

After a while, Paul appeared tired and listless. He let his hooked stick slip to the pavement. The light left his eyes. Collin began to worry. When had the other boy eaten? Collin dared not ask, because he sensed the other boy's pride. That evening he told Tyndale about Paul, and was delighted at Tyndale's interest.

The next day Tyndale talked to Paul while Collin browsed at a bookseller's stall. In a few minutes Tyndale came up. "We're going with Paul to where he lives. He says there's someone sick down there."

Paul had perked up. Bright and alert, he sped light-footed through the crooked streets at a pace that left Collin breathless. Paul stopped at a run-down wharf. Half-open bales of cargo lay stacked in every direction. The odors of spoiled food and dead fish rose from the river.

"Here we are. They don't use this anymore—not after the ship sank." Paul pointed to a tunnel made of tumbled barrels. "She—she's in there."

William Tyndale's kind expression did not change. Collin tried to look as if he too were accustomed to a house made of boxes and barrels.

Paul went ahead. "I've got a friend with me," he called. "He's a preacher, and he's going to help you get well."

Inside the air was unbearably close. Collin could just make out the figure of Paul stooping to re-arrange some rags around a woman lying in the corner. The woman murmured something. Collin could see a thin, lined face. The woman brushed back a few wisps of hair that had come loose under her tight bonnet.

"I'm Amy Blake," she said in a thick accent. Collin saw that she was too ill to speak above a hoarse whisper. "I'm from Germany. Paul's father would be proud of him, the way he earns our keep. We don't owe a farthing to anybody. Now I'm going to die. What will become of Paul?"

She closed her eyes. Collin saw tears glisten below her lashes. Tyndale spoke to her in German. Mrs. Blake brightened at once. The two talked for several minutes. Finally Tyndale rose to leave. "We'll take you to our inn," he said in English.

Mrs. Blake shook her head. "I'll never leave here. It's my home. My husband brought me here from Germany. He drowned when the ship sank, but he saved ten men, and they're all alive to this day. I'll never leave this place."

Every day Tyndale brought food to Mrs. Blake, and Collin would come in later with Paul. The neighborhood learned of Mrs. Blake's illness and soon women friends bustled in and out.

"We didn't know—we just didn't know she was ill," one explained. "Mrs. Blake has so much pride, you know. But her husband saved mine from drowning, and neither I nor the others he saved will forget that."

It was not long before the whole neighborhood knew William Tyndale. They talked of his comforting words, his prayers, and his help. Some declared that without William Tyndale's prayers, Mrs. Blake would have died. Collin saw the people's sympathy when Tyndale spoke of his plan to translate the Bible into English so that they could all read it. Everyone warned him of the penalty.

"We know the ways of the church. You're taking your life in your hands," more than one told him, "but if you finish it, send it to us and we'll see that it is distributed."

William Tyndale smiled and thanked them, but Collin saw that he was just being courteous. Paul must have noticed that Tyndale was not really accepting the offer. One day Paul's eyes danced with more mischief than usual. "Sir William, we have ways of knowing about what's going to happen ahead of time." He and Collin took Tyndale to the cathedral. "Now, watch."

Once again Paul whistled his odd whistle. It was echoed from every corner. A grin of understanding crossed Tyndale's face. "I believe you," he told Paul. "That's quite a spy system."

A few days later Paul sent a message to Tyndale through Collin. "Tell him he's going to get a summons to the bishop's palace. I just got word this morning. One of our people holds the bishop's horses, and he heard some people talking about it."

Paul's prediction came true. At the inn a message had been left with the innkeeper, who was almost bug-eyed with awe.

"Such fine livery—the horses were all in gold—every inch of them, and they stopped in front of my inn. Oh, it has been a wonderful day. The neighborhood has never seen anything like it."

"Yes, yes, but where is the message?" Tyndale asked.

"Oh, right here, Sir William, right here. You can be sure I kept it safely."

The innkeeper babbled on, while Tyndale read and reread the paper. "Paul was right," he told Collin. "You can go with me. I'll take the Greek translation to show the bishop." He hummed to himself. "Should I take anything else to show I'm capable of translating? No," he answered himself. "All that in due time."

The day of the appointment seemed long in coming. In the anteroom of the palace, the room was filled with petitioners. When an assistant ushered Tyndale and Collin through to the main chamber, a murmur of disappointment went through the crowd. Collin sensed that they were asking themselves and each other what favor Tyndale had with the bishop to be allowed to see him first.

Collin trembled with awe at the sight of the richly robed bishop, who sat in an ornate chair before a long, polished table. At first Collin could only stare at the huge signet ring on the bishop's forefinger. When he dared to look at the bishop's stern, thoughtful face, Collin suddenly felt terrified and weak in the

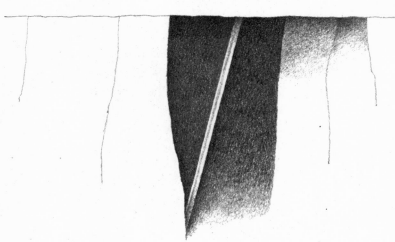

*Bishop Tonstall*

knees. Bishop Tonstall did not even glance at Collin. He waved away the letters of introduction William Tyndale pulled out.

"No, no, Tyndale. Your recommendations are the highest, and your scholarship is impeccable. You seem to have quite a bit of influence among the people wherever you go. Such influence can be dangerous. Just what are you doing here in London?"

When Tyndale explained, Bishop Tonstall slumped back in his heavily carved chair and drummed his fingers on the arms. "Alas, Tyndale, my house is full. I have now more people than I can employ."

Collin saw Tyndale's shoulders sag with disappointment.

"Besides," the bishop added, "your preaching is stirring up the people. Do you think it wise to give them an appetite for something forbidden?"

"Should a Bible in their own tongue be forbidden the people?" Tyndale countered.

A mottled crimson flooded the bishop's face. He drummed his fingers again and then placed the tips together. "Look at that man Luther. His works are spreading like the plague. Today he calls for the abolition of the mass; tomorrow he will ask for the abolition of Jesus Christ."

Collin was not quite sure what the bishop meant, but he understood the hostile tone.

Tyndale paced in front of the long table. "The church has exalted its own honor above the king and above God Himself. The church would rather put forth a thousand books inscribed with false learning than see that the Scriptures come to light for the lay people."

58

The bishop fingered his signet ring. "Have you forgotten the Constitution of Arundel in 1408?"

Tyndale broke in hotly. "It prohibited unauthorized versions of the Scriptures, but the king himself will be willing to authorize my version."

"What makes you so sure?" Bishop Tonstall now toyed with a gold paper weight on the table.

"Because God's authority is higher than the king's." Tyndale breathed fast as he said the words. Collin stiffened with dread. Would Tyndale begin to pound the bishop's table in his excitement?

"It is dangerous—very dangerous—to criticize existing conditions," the bishop murmured. "The church service as we now know it has been in existence hundreds of years. I think we can be sure it will continue to exist—in Latin—for hundreds of years in the future." He rang a tiny golden bell. At once the door opened and John Tisen entered. His red beard had never seemed more hateful to Collin. Teacher and ex-student stared at each other; then Tisen ushered out Tyndale and Collin. No one spoke.

Collin had never seen Tyndale so plunged in gloom. All the way to the inn, the scene at the bishop's palace went through Collin's mind. He knew Tyndale too must have reviewed over and over what had taken place.

At the inn, the innkeeper ran out to meet them. "You have a visitor—a very important man."

A businessman with fur lapels on his cloak hurried out with hands outstretched.

"So, you're Sir William. I've been meaning to come see you for several weeks. I'm Humphrey Monmouth."

"The merchant?" Tyndale all but gasped the words.

"I've heard of you from my brother. He's a merchant here in town, but not as well known as you."

"I've been hearing your services—I go three miles just to listen to your sermons," Humphrey Monmouth said. "You are the man of our times. I marvel that you can be such a scholar and yet be so direct and understandable. What are your plans for the future?"

Collin listened to Tyndale pour out the story of his many weeks of waiting, and how the Bishop of London had turned down Tyndale's request for a position in his palace.

"He refused?" Humphrey Monmouth asked, his head cocked on one side. "That's understandable. He has to stay on the right side of Cardinal Wolsey, you know, and I have a feeling that the cardinal would not approve of all you plan. But I want you to live at my house. I shall see to it that you need not worry about earning a living. Your mission is of utmost importance to England. I shall be very proud to have you as my guest—and your page, too, of course." Humphrey Monmouth smiled down at Collin.

Within a short time, Collin felt at home in Humphrey Monmouth's well-furnished house. William Tyndale chose an attic room for his study and worked on his translations for many hours a day. In the mornings, Collin studied the lessons Tyndale assigned him and spent the afternoons with Paul at the cathedral. He had persuaded Paul to teach him German, but Collin had a plan other than fleecing people with the language. Someday Tyndale might want to visit Martin Luther in Germany, and Collin wanted to understand what the two men would say. But it was a secret desire. He did not even tell Paul.

o   o   o

One day Collin came to the cathedral to find Paul, but his friend was not in sight. A few minutes later, Paul ran up, his face pinched with worry. "I just found out something terrible. Hurry, and tell Sir William." Paul grabbed Collin's arm and shook it.

"Tell him what?"

Paul gasped out the words. "They're going to set Humphrey Monmouth's house on fire and burn up all those manuscripts—and they hope Sir William will be burned, too." Paul pranced in agony. "Go tell him. I'll see if I can find out any more." Paul disappeared.

Collin darted through the streets, a lump of fear rising in his throat. Long before he reached the house, he saw a billow of smoke. Fire—the dread of every person in London—mounted in a column from the ground floor of Humphrey Monmouth's house and licked at the attic room where William Tyndale sat translating the Bible. Collin well knew Tyndale would be so busy he would not even notice the flames until too late. Even as he thought, Collin saw the white smoke part and a shaft a cruel red flame dart upward.

Chapter **6**

# *Inspired Flight*

Collin forced his way through a group of women clustered at a safe distance from the burning house. He could feel the heat of the red-orange flames shooting up between puffs of dull gray smoke. Men hauled furniture out of the ground floor. Others formed a bucket brigade, led by Humphrey Monmouth, who had taken off his fine cloak and rolled up the sleeves of his white shirt. On the roofs of neighboring houses children clambered through dormer windows and dabbed at sparks with wet cloths.

Collin stood on tiptoe, trying to catch a glimpse of the attic room where Tyndale worked. It occurred to him that Tyndale might have gone on some errand of mercy, as he often did in the afternoon. Relieved at the thought, Collin searched the faces of the crowd. Which one of these people would have told church authorities about Tyndale's whereabouts? Could it be the carpenter with his horny hands and leather apron split and fastened about the knees? Or was it the tailor, a man of spare form, sallow face, and quick eye? Or perhaps it was Humphrey Monmouth's closest neighbor, a merchant in long gown of sober cut, square cap, and golden chain.

One man stood out above all. Tall, and clothed from head to foot in a thick brown robe, he moved quickly from one person to another, holding out trinkets. Collin watched a woman glance at the tall man's hand, cross herself, and draw a coin from the purse at her waist.

"It's a hair from the head of a dead saint," the tall man said, bending toward the woman. His robe gaped open, and Collin saw a checkered doublet of green, red, and white. No real churchman would wear clothes like that, Collin told himself. He edged closer and listened to the tall man's whine.

"This will protect you and your family from the curse of fire," the robed man said to a woman. She bought a relic. Soon he had sold a dozen.

A cheer broke out from the bucket brigade. Only a wisp of smoke drifted upward. Collin sniffed the smell of wet, burned wood and damp whitewash.

Humphrey Monmouth, his face blackened, his fine white shirt torn and muddy, peered into the house. His wife and children came up and stood with him, silent and downcast.

A bystander shouted and pointed upward. Someone was unlatching the dormer window.

"Look! There's a man up there," someone said

William Tyndale, his hand still on the latch, looked out on the crowd below. "I thought I smelled smoke. Is there a fire somewhere?"

There was a gasp of astonishment from the crowd. "Didn't you know the house was on fire?"

Tyndale looked puzzled. "No. I was busy with my book."

For a moment the crowd was silent. Then a roar of laughter burst forth. People pounded each other on the back, repeating, "He was busy—too busy to notice the house was on fire."

"Who is that man?" Collin heard the tall man in brown robes ask.

"That's William Tyndale," one of the bucket brigade answered. "He's a preacher. He prayed over my sick daughter last week and now she is up and well. He's going to bring the Scriptures to us in our own language."

At these words the tall man jerked to attention and questioned one after another about William Tyndale. Everyone praised Tyndale.

A woman ran up to the tall man, waving the saint's relic she had bought. "You cheat, you! This is not the hair of a saint. If it isn't a hair off a horse's tail, may I burn for it."

Others examined their relics and began to mutter. Without another word, the brown-robed man darted through the crowd and disappeared. Collin was convinced now that the man must be a spy. Why would he have asked so many questions? It was plain, too, that the man was a scamp. Perhaps even now he was telling the church authorities about Tyndale's influence on the people.

Now that the danger and excitement of the fire had died, the crowd drifted away. Some marveled at Tyndale's escape from suffocation. Others agreed. Collin could hear the name *Tyndale* on many lips.

He followed Humphrey Monmouth and his family into the back room of the house. Monmouth examined a pile of charred cloth.

"Did someone deliver a bale of goods today?"

Collin could tell from Mrs. Monmouth's startled face that something of the kind had happened. Her pale blue eyes widened. "Yes. Two strange men came. One said they were from the wharf—said you would understand what the cloth was for. I didn't give it a second thought. The other man didn't say anything. He was young, with a fiery red beard and dark red hair—very odd."

Collin's heart lurched. Only one man in London looked like that—John Tisen. Was he taking out a personal vengeance on William Tyndale, his former teacher? Or was this part of his work for Cardinal Wolsey, the dreaded High Chancellor of England?

Humphrey Monmouth fingered the charred cloth. "Whoever the man was, he spoke with a double tongue. I understand very well what he means." Monmouth had a faraway look. "We must act quickly, this very night."

In the cleaning up that followed, Collin had no chance to ask what Humphrey Monmouth meant. Collin went to bed hours later, tired to the bone. It seemed to him that he had hardly touched the pillow when he was awakened by William Tyndale.

"Get up and dress," Tyndale whispered. "Then come downstairs."

Wide awake in a instant, Collin obeyed. Monmouth and Tyndale were waiting for him on the first floor. Without a word, they ushered him outside and started down the dark streets at almost a run. Collin did not dare ask the two men where they were going.

At a wharf piled high with bundles, crates, and bales, Humphrey Monmouth led the way into a warehouse. Several bulky figures moved toward them. Collin shivered. His hair prickled along his neck. He fought a panickly impulse to run—he didn't know where or why. He felt as if spies were crouched in every pocket of darkness along the wharf.

"There you are," a man said in a low, relieved tone. "All the rest of us are here. We were beginning to wonder if it was already too late."

Someone lit a candle. By its flickering light Collin saw six or seven merchants in fur-lined cloaks. Tyndale went quickly to one, a man half a head taller than he, with a long slender face. The two clasped hands.

"Yes, Sir William, I notified your brother," Humphrey Monmouth said. "John has pledged his help."

"I knew he would," Tyndale said, smiling. "Only I'm not sure just what help is needed."

Collin started with surprise and impatience. Couldn't Tyndale understand that his life was in danger? Did he think the fire was just an accident? Then Collin realized he had not had a chance to tell Tyndale how Paul's friends had overheard the plot.

Humphrey Monmouth sat on a counter and motioned to the others to sit on bales of goods. "There is no doubt in my mind that Sir William is being persecuted by the church."

Tyndale's brother John jumped up. "With Sir William's brilliant reputation at Oxford and Cambridge, I don't think the church would dare take any drastic step. Annoy him, yes; even threaten him,

66

but I don't believe it will go farther than that."

"You don't?" Humphrey Monmouth was polite but firm. "Two years ago, as you know, Cardinal Wolsey ordered all Lutheran literature to be turned in, but Luther's books haven't stopped coming. The cardinal is doubling, tripling his spy system." Monmouth told the others about the fire. "If Sir William prints an English Bible, sooner or later he will pay for it—with his life."

There was a meaningful silence. An almost uncontrollable trembling seized Collin. He watched the flickering shadows cast by the candle. What lay in the dark corners behind the merchants? Perhaps a church spy was listening and identifying every person at the meeting. Collin tried not to think of the red-bearded John Tisen.

"Do you feel you must go on with this translation?" Tyndale's brother asked in a respectful voice.

"Yes," William Tyndale said. "Christ commanded His disciples to publish His last will and testament. He did not say to hand it out in Latin; He said to give it to all people. What Luther did for the German people, with God's help, I shall do for the English. I shall never alter one syllable of the Scriptures against my conscience."

The candle sputtered, casting shadows on the white, strained faces of the merchants.

Humphrey Monmouth put his arm around Sir William's shoulders. "Your work will light a candle which will never be put out, and I pledge my help."

"I, too," the others echoed one by one.

"Then first let us advance the money that will

67

allow Sir William to translate the Bible without worrying about his daily bread," Humphrey Monmouth proposed.

Everyone agreed. Tyndale bowed his thanks. "I am now beginning to see the pattern of things to come," he said, "spied on, never free. My translation will offend the church, but I pray that the King of England will see the light." Tyndale's voice deepened and his jaw muscles tightened. "There was not room for me in my lord of London's palace, and I see now there is no place for me in all England."

Again a silence filled the room. Collin stared at the candle flame. It seemed to him that Tyndale himself had become the tiny flame that was the only light in a world of shadows, fear, and treachery. Collin resolved to stay with Tyndale no matter what happened. At once he felt a curious lightheartedness and gladness. He looked boldly at the dark corners of the warehouse room and made a new discovery. There was nothing frightening about mere shadows.

"Yes, Sir William," Humphrey Monmouth was saying, "you must go to the continent. What is forbidden in one part can be done safely in another."

William Tyndale smiled. "But they burn books abroad, and fire is not a theological argument."

Humphrey Monmouth did not laugh at Tyndale's joke. "Go to Germany. The art of printing is advanced there. You'll be working in a language few understand, and there will be less chance of spies finding you."

John Tyndale broke in. "As soon as you have it printed, you can smuggle it here. A few books in a bale of cloth, a few more in a barrel of flour—"

"Yes," a merchant agreed, chuckling. "William Tyndale, merchant of Bibles—or rather, Bible smuggler. You didn't learn that at Oxford, did you?"

The talk became light banter for a moment. Collin drowsed, wondering why he had been brought to the meeting.

Humphrey Monmouth rapped for attention. "Sir William, you must leave tomorrow morning for the continent."

This news startled Collin into excited wakefulness. A buoyant expectation bubbled up within him, and he itched for the trip to begin.

"One more thing, Sir William," Monmouth said. "It will be better for you to use another name."

Tyndale agreed. "I'll use a family name—Hutchins," he said. "If I took a strange name, I might forget it."

Humphrey Monmouth opened the warehouse door and looked outside. "It will soon be dawn, and there must be no sign of a meeting here. Now, Sir William, let me give you a final warning. Keep your work secret. Don't let people find out how much you know. Of course, you can't disguise your Oxford accent, but don't be lured into discussions of the church and its problems. You sometimes get carried away, you know."

Tyndale nodded in all meekness.

"You'll need more suitable clothes than your scholar's robes," Monmouth went on.

"Here. Exchange with me." John Tyndale took off his fur-lined cloak and exchanged it for his brother's long robe. "Now you can be a prosperous merchant looking for markets on the continent."

The next morning at the dock, Tyndale appeared to be a merchant to Collin's way of thinking. They lined up with other passengers ready to board the little sailing vessel. In spite of his lack of sleep, Collin looked and listened with interest, while the crew made ready to cast off.

When the passengers were all aboard, the captain called, "Haul the bowline. Veer the sheet."

The prompt answer drifted over the breeze. "It shall be done."

Sails bellied out before the wind. The forecastle pointed toward unknown land. Collin looked back at the wharf, trying to keep his feet steady on deck. Tyndale, with strangely white face, clung to the rail with both hands and gazed as if he could not get his fill.

"Oh, sir, isn't it exciting to sail like this?" Collin pounded the rail in his excitement. "Just think, this is my first trip on water."

Tyndale still looked at the land. "It is my first trip, too—and my last," he added in an undertone.

For a long time, Collin watched the water, feeling the wind push and tip the boat. A little later the wind stirred up waves and whistled so sharply in Collin's ears that he turned to find shelter. As he did so, a tall man in green and white checkered doublet, slightly stoop-shouldered, came toward them. At once all of Collin's excitement turned into dismay. The man was the one who had sold relics the day before at the fire—the one who had asked so many questions about Tyndale.

With a sinking sensation in his stomach, Collin

realized he had forgotten to tell William Tyndale about the spying relic seller. How could he have forgotten such important news?

The man came closer. His long arms curved like barrel staves. Collin stared. Was the man trying to keep his balance, or did he have a more sinister purpose?

"This ship is a perilous horse to ride," the stranger said to Tyndale.

The ship tilted. The stranger's outstretched arms closed around William Tyndale. It would take only a shove of the stranger's powerful hand and Tyndale would be knocked overboard. In the split second of realization, Collin saw one thing he could do. If it failed, all three would go overboard. Collin crouched, a choked prayer on his lips.

Chapter 7

# Two Strangers

Collin gasped a warning to William Tyndale, hurled himself on the stranger's back, and clawed at the man's large hands. The next instant the deck rose and jarred Collin's shoulder, but he kept tight hold of the man's neck. His opponent did not fight back, and Collin loosened his grip. The man sank to the deck gasping out a phrase in Latin.

With an exclamation of surprise, William Tyndale helped the stranger to his feet. The man stared at Collin in reproachful surprise. "What did you do that for? Couldn't you see that I had lost my balance?"

He looked so woebegone that Collin choked back a laugh. No one as loose-jointed and ridiculous-looking as this man could be a threat.

The stranger addressed Tyndale. "I was just coming over to ask your advice about something, when the ship listed and your boy there threw himself on me."

Tydale raised his eyebrows in a questioning way and looked at Collin.

"I—I'm sorry," Collin said, gulping. "I thought—"

He did not finish. It would sound foolish to say now that he thought the stranger was going to throw William Tyndale overboard.

"You see," the man went on, "Mr.—Mr.—" He waited for the name.

With a slight frown of annoyance, Tyndale said coolly, "Hutchins is the name."

"Ah, yes, Mr. Hutchins. I saw at once that you are a successful merchant. I'm a good judge of people, and I said to myself, Now look at his man. He's a success and I'm a failure. Perhaps he can advise me how to get hold of some money—I mean earn it, of course." The stranger leaned on the rail and clasped his large hands. His glance traveled up and down Tyndale's fine cloak. "Perhaps you could use someone to write letters of business for you."

All of Collin's former doubts flooded his mind. Collin hoped Tyndale would brush the man off, but he could see that Tyndale was curious.

"I have many qualifications, Mr. Hutchins," the man went on. "I know languages—German, Latin, and Greek."

Tyndale's eyes sparkled with interest. Collin squirmed with misgivings. Why would this strange man name the very languages Tyndale was working with in his translation of the Bible? Yet if he were a spy hired by Cardinal Wolsey, would he grin so foolishly and wave his hands about? The man's babbling eagerness irritated Collin.

"I said to myself when I saw you, Mr. Hutchins, that you're a man I'd like to be around—a prosperous gentleman merchant who makes a lot of money and would be willing to share it with poor

73

scholars like me. I'd earn it, of course. You see, I have no money." The stranger pulled out an empty bag and waved it. "I used all I earned in England to pay my fare on this ship."

Collin wanted to cry out that he had seen the man at the fire selling fake relics, but he curbed his impulse.

Tyndale stared out over the choppy waters of the channel.

"Is there going to be a storm, Sir William?" Collin asked. He could have bitten his tongue for giving away Tyndale's first name and honorary title.

"William?" The man gave a little spring and kicked his heels. "My name's William, too—William Roye." Roye grinned a thank-you to Collin, leaned forward, and spoke in a confidential tone. "You must have many letters to write, Sir William."

Tyndale gazed at Roye, as if sounding him out. Collin had the feeling that Tyndale was praying for guidance. At last Tyndale sighed. He bowed his head in a gesture of helplessness and resignation.

"I would like to know where you received your education." he said. "It seems unusual for a man —ah—in your position to know three languages."

"Not unusual in the least," Roye said. "You see, I was a monk."

"A monk!" Tyndale jumped back as if he had stepped on a snake. "And why, may I ask, aren't you a monk any longer?"

Roye shuddered and rolled his eyes to the sky. "It was the hair shirt. Abominable thing. If it had either hurt or itched, I would have been able to stand it. But it did both. I ran away."

74

Tyndale half smiled. "So God has sent a runaway monk to be my helper."

Roye's large mouth drooped. "It doesn't sound good when you put it that way. How about Martin Luther? He was a monk and he made his way in the world."

Tyndale did not answer.

"Sir William—" Roye whined the name in a sulky voice. "I help scholars prepare manuscripts, and I would do it again, but it doesn't pay enough. That's why I thought I'd attach myself to a prosperous merchant like yourself."

While Collin listened, he was thinking ahead. Maybe Roye would turn them in to the church authorities as soon as the ship reached shore. Cardinal Wolsey's agents could be anyplace. Collin hoped Tyndale would not talk anymore, but he saw that Tyndale had just begun.

"And what if I told you I am not what you think I am?" Tyndale was saying. "I'm a runaway, too, and in disguise."

Roye stretched his neck in amazement. He seemed unable to turn his gaze away from the fur-lined lapels of Tyndale's cloak. "But that's a fine garment you're wearing."

"It's my brother's."

"Does he have money?" Roye asked.

"He's what you like to call a prosperous mercant."

"Where is he?"

"In England," Tyndale said.

Roye reflected. "I don't think I'd better go back to England for a while." After a moment he asked,

75

"Why are you in disguise?"

"Because of the work I'm doing," Tyndale said. "It requires the use of Latin, Greek, and German books."

A strange, crafty expression, blended of fear and interest, crossed Roye's face. "There is only one kind of work that involves three languages. Would you be translating something?"

"Yes."

Collin groaned in dismay. Roye drummed his fingers on the rail. "Is this translation for or against the church?"

"It is for the true church," Tyndale said.

Roye pondered in silence for a moment. "Where is this true church you mentioned?" he asked with nervous caution.

"In the hearts of men who are redeemed."

"Who are these?"

"No one can say. A man can be judged only by his actions, and these, however good, may not spring from the heart. Only God knows the names of His true churchmen."

"I don't think much of the church at Rome," Roye said, with a sly glance.

"Then you aren't one of Cardinal Wolsey's spies?" Collin blurted the question before he thought.

"The cardinal's spy?" Roye repeated in bewilderment. "No, no, I swear it, Sir William, believe me. I am a runaway monk. If the church captures me, I'll be punished. I want to save my skin, and I want to get ahead in the world, too. A person can't live without money. Try me out, Sir William. Find out what I know."

*Tyndale, Collin, and Roye approaching Hamburg.*

Tyndale addressed Roye in Latin, Greek, and German. To Collin's secret envy, the ex-monk answered fluently in all three.

Tyndale stared over the water for a long time. The waves had quieted and the ship skimmed the waves at an even keel. "Very well," Tyndale said. "You may help me."

Roye kicked his heels and popped into the air in such a loose-jointed fashion Collin burst into laughter.

"Sir William, you will not regret your choice," Roye said. "What are you translating—one of the old church fathers, no doubt?"

"I am translating the Bible into English."

Roye stepped back. He opened and closed his mouth several times, rolled his eyes, and then seemed to recover himself. "Now, just what will my salary be—and would you advance me a little?"

"We'll discuss your salary when we are settled in Hamburg," Tyndale said.

Crestfallen, Roye shrugged consent. He appeared alternately glum and elated during the rest of the trip to Germany. Collin watched him swagger about the ship, putting on airs before the other passengers. Roye both amused and irritated Collin.

❀ ❀ ❀

Hamburg was not a bit like London. It was threaded by canals and bordered by gabled warehouses rising sheer from the side of the water. High above the highest building, church spires pointed upward. To Collin, they seemed like warning fingers.

Roye nodded toward the church. "It's everywhere. You can never get away from it."

The church seemed to follow them to the edge of town, where Tyndale hunted for the address of friends. He knocked at the door of a tall, narrow house, showed a letter of introduction to a maid, and stepped back waiting. Collin stood in uneasy silence, watching Roye, who paced back and forth.

A young man ran to the door. "I'm Matthias von Emersen," he said, grasping Tyndale's hand in both of his. "Do come in." He ushered the group into a sitting room where his family sat. All listened with eager interest while Tyndale told of his plan to translate the Bible into English. All agreed that it was better to keep such plans secret. "The church—the church," they murmured and shook their heads.

"Are you using the Hebrew Scriptures?" Matthias von Emersen asked Tyndale.

"I'm not too strong in that language," Tyndale said. "I wish I were."

Matthias put both hands on Tyndale's shoulders. "Then you must go to Wittenberg and learn Hebrew there. You can talk to Martin Luther, too."

Tyndale's eyes gleamed and his long face lit up with excitement. Collin could see that Tyndale needed only a little encouragement to travel on to Wittenberg.

"Yes, that's the only thing to do," Matthias continued. "Send Roye on ahead. A man and a boy traveling will create less curiosity than two men and a boy. I know enough about your English cardinal to know his agents will try to track you down."

When the plans were completed, Tyndale counted

out expense money for Roye's trip to Wittenberg. "Don't chatter to strangers about your work with me," he warned.

Roye looked pained. "I know well how to keep out of trouble with the church. Don't forget that I was once a monk." He added in a brighter tone, "I'll leave early tomorrow morning."

But Roye did not wait, Collin discovered the next day. Sometime in the middle of the night he skipped out.

William Tyndale sighed and shook his head. "I shouldn't have given him any money," he told everyone at breakfast. "That is his great weakness. But he is an excellent scholar, and with his help I could have finished the translation by next year."

Tyndale did not mention Roye on the way to Wittenberg. Collin, once more on horseback, worried about Roye. Would he betray Tyndale for money? The friendly German people eased his mind. No one asked questions. Everyone seemed happy to lodge the travelers.

A few miles from Wittenberg, Tyndale turned the horses to a less traveled road and continued until they came to a small inn. The landlady opened the door. Her face, framed by the stiff linen fold of her wimple, was swollen, and her eyes were red-rimmed. She dabbed at her eyes with the corner of a clean apron and tried to smile.

"God be with you here," Tyndale said in greeting.

The landlady burst into sobs.

Tyndale stepped toward her. "Can I help you?"

"Oh, sir, it's my daughter. She has the sweating sickness—it's fatal, you know—and she with four small children." The landlady put a trembling hand to her mouth. "But do come in and welcome. I see you are a gentleman."

"If you would like me to, I will pray with your daughter," Tyndale said. "In my country I am an ordained preacher."

"Oh, would you?" Joy and hope transfigured the woman's plain face. Collin's throat tightened in sympathy.

"Of course. Collin, here, will watch for travelers." The landlady nodded, smiling. "He need only say I'll be back soon." She motioned Tyndale to the rear of the inn toward a hallway.

A little later, Collin found out what Tyndale, as God's instrument, had accomplished. The landlady came in saying over and over, "It is a miracle. With my own eyes I saw the fever pass from her." She ran to stir up the fire. "Anything in my house is yours, sir. My inn is small and not on the main road, but I must say travelers return here when they come this way. Now, what will you have for supper?"

"That can wait," Tyndale said. "First, we must tend to the horses."

"Oh, I have a groom who does that," the landlady said.

Tyndale was firm. "I have some important papers and books packed, and I prefer to handle them myself." At the doorway he stopped short with an exclamation of surprise. Collin ran up and looked out.

The landlady's groom must have spilled the saddlebags. Papers and books lay strewn on the ground. The groom stood wringing his hands. Collin

81

wondered why Tyndale did not run out at once. Then he saw why.

A man whom Collin had not seen at first straightened up. He was a tall man clothed entirely in red, from hose and doublet to red cap. A sword hung at his side. As Collin watched, the man picked up Luther's New Testament, a book Collin recognized even from that distance.

The stranger's plump face, with a hint of double chin, looked purposeful. He spoke to the groom, poked among the papers and books for a moment, and then strode toward the inn, still carrying Luther's New Testament. Large and imposing, he held himself so straight that he seemed to bend backward. At each step he stroked his long sword, a sight that sent shudders of terror down Collin's spine.

## Chapter 8

## *Unseen Visitors*

William Tyndale started outside, but Collin clung to him. "Oh, Sir William, don't go out there. It must be one of Cardinal Wolsey's spies. Look at his sword. He'll kill us."

"I shall not leave my manuscript out there," Tyndale said.

The landlady clutched at Tyndale's cloak. "I don't know what this all means, but you saved my daughter's life. Go hide in the stable. I'll take care of this man."

Tyndale shook himself free. "My manuscript is worth more than my life."

The landlady pointed to a scullion's smock hanging near the fireplace. "Then at least put on this smock. I have a chicken ready for the spit. You can turn it and hear for yourself what the man intends to do. I'll get your manuscript myself."

Tyndale slipped into the smock and began to twirl the spit with frenzied speed.

"Not too fast," the landlady warned in a whisper. She handed Collin some clean linens. "Set the table there by the window. I'll have the groom bring the papers and books into the kitchen."

She whisked out the back way. The tall stranger entered, and it seemed to Collin that the man filled the doorway. Collin was baffled by the kind, earnest look on the plump face. Somehow this person did not look like a swordsman.

The stranger in red sat down by the window and laid the book on the table. "Who owns Martin Luther's New Testament?" he asked Collin.

Collin could not keep his gaze off the sword. He smoothed the tablecloth, fighting waves of terror. His hands shook and his tongue stuck to the roof of his mouth. "Some—someone came earlier on horseback," he said, jerking out the words. "He'll be back later."

The stranger's face fell. "I very much want to meet the man who travels with this book." He glanced toward the fireplace. "Is that chicken ready to eat?"

William Tyndale hunched over and spun the spit faster than before.

"I don't know. The landlady will be right back, sir." Collin said.

The landlady hurried in, curtsying and apologizing. When the chicken was ready, William Tyndale unhooked the spit with such awkwardness that the chicken fell onto the hot coals. The landlady was at his side in one jump. She shook her fist in Tyndale's face. "You clumsy oaf. Back to the kitchen with you." She pushed him out of the dining room, beckoning Collin to follow.

In the kitchen Tyndale slumped on a high stool. "I'll pay for the chicken," he said in humble tones.

"You'll do nothing of the sort," the landlady said, kindly. "I just scolded you in order to get you out

of the dining room. Here are your books and papers."
She pointed toward a neat pile on the table.

Tyndale leafed through the papers with intent
eagerness. "They're all here," he said, smiling. "I
would hate to do all this work over again." He rest-
ed one hand on the manuscript. "I think the boy
and I had better go on a little farther tonight.
We'll pay you for a night's lodging, anyway, because of all the trouble you've had on my account."

The landlady's eyes filled with tears. Collin saw
that she had not forgotten for a moment what
Tyndale had done for her daughter.

"Indeed you'll not pay a cent. I can put you in a
back room and you can be on your way by the first
streak of dawn, and no one the wiser."

A booming voice from the doorway made all of
them jump.

"Is there some trouble in this house?" The stranger
in red came straight toward the book-laden table.
With a look of puzzlement and curiosity, he stared
at Tyndale. "Perhaps the book I brought inside
belongs here, too," he said.

"Yes, it does." There was defiance in Tyndale's
voice, and Collin's muscles tensed. Why was the
stranger so insistent?

"I perceive by your accent that you are from
England," the stranger said. "Perhaps you could tell
me—is the name Martin Luther well known in that
country?"

Collin saw a slight tremor in Tyndale's hands.
He knew well that Tyndale was tempted to talk.

"His name is a household word," Tyndale admitted.

The stranger beamed. Then a shadow crossed his plump face. "In what way do you mean? What do people think of Luther there?"

Tyndale hesitated. Collin clenched his fists, hoping Tyndale would not talk too much.

"There are many opinions about Martin Luther," Tyndale said. "Some cannot praise him enough. Some, particularly the clergy, damn him as a heretic."

The stranger grunted then straightened up and spoke in an excited manner. "Should any cry out that Luther is a heretic, I am certain he cares but little for their clamors. Such men as accuse him have never tasted the Bible. But Luther has cleared the stumps and stones out of the way so that others may read the Scriptures without hindrance."

"Do you by any chance know Luther?" Tyndale asked. "I am hoping to meet him in Wittenberg."

The stranger in red hesitated, reddened, clenched his fists, and then laughed aloud. "You have already met him," he said bowing.

"You mean you're Martin Luther himself?" Collin breathed the words in such disbelief, wonderment, and shock, that both men laughed.

The two men began to talk at the same time. They laughed, excused themselves, and started again. The words poured out in a flood of excited exchange. When Tyndale spoke of translating the Bible into English, Martin Luther leaned toward him and waggled a finger in warning. "Translating is not everybody's gift. It demands a pious, true, industrious, Christian, learned, experienced, and practiced heart."

Tyndale bowed his head humbly.

"I found it a laborious task to force Hebrew writers to talk German," Martin Luther went on. "It was as if a nightingale had to give up its own sweet melody and imitate the song of the cuckoo."

Tyndale agreed. "Many have told me the English tongue is too clumsy," he said, "but I always ask them, 'Has not God made the English tongue as well as others?'"

Martin Luther chuckled. "Yes, but be sure you do not get your English from the Latin. You must get it from the mother in the house, the child in the street, and the common man in the marketplace."

Tyndale's face became sad. "But I am exiled from England. I shall never again hear the English mother, the English child, or the English laborer."

The wistfulness in his voice brought a lump of sympathy to Collin's throat.

Martin Luther was silent for a moment. "If this work be of God, nothing on earth will stop it."

The men must have talked the night away. The next thing Collin knew, Tyndale was shaking him by the shoulder and urging him to dress. Collin was bewildered. He could not remember even going to bed.

"Martin Luther has gone on alone," Tyndale told Collin. "He agrees that we must keep in hiding, even though Wittenberg is liberal in its religious views."

A few hours later, Collin and Tyndale dismounted at the city gates of Wittenberg and led their horses to the deputy in charge.

87

"What is your business here?" the deputy asked.

"Student at the university."

The deputy motioned them through. Ahead, not far from the gates, a group of townspeople had gathered, watching the entrance.

Their stares made Collin uncomfortable. "Do they know you're coming?" he whispered to William Tyndale. "What are they waiting for?"

Three horsemen galloped in and dismounted. A man dressed in black with a long gold chain around his neck pushed his way past Collin and Tyndale. The deputy at the gate bowed and bawled out in loud tones, "The grace of God and of the holy father is at our gates."

A crowd of people surged forward. Some held up lighted tapers. Others beat drums. Still others rang bells.

A carriage entered the arched gateway and drew up beside the three horsemen. One of the riders opened the carriage door. A man in brown robes stepped out, bearing before him a blue velvet cushion with a scroll fastened on cloth of gold. Murmurs of awe came from the townspeople. Collin, too, exclaimed, and William Tyndale groaned. There was no mistaking the tall, awkward figure of William Roye.

Roye glanced at them, paled, and hurried toward the sound of blowing horns.

A glimmer of understanding came to Collin. "He's selling relics again, isn't he, Sir William?"

They watched a second man step out of the carriage, holding a large, wooden cross in front of him.

"He's got a partner," Collin whispered. He and Tyndale followed the procession to the market square

88

and listened to Roye harangue the people. "Good folks, do not crowd so much," Roye said. "Make way for those who have money. We will afterward endeavor to satisfy those who have none."

Tyndale whispered to Collin, "His tongue not only would make fools go mad but also would deceive the wisest—at first sight and acquaintance of him."

"Here is the comb of the cock that crowed at the house of Pilate," Roye called out. "And here is a piece of planking from Noah's ark. I have the very pebble David used to slay the giant Goliath. Don't crowd, don't crowd, good folk. There is enough for all."

Tyndale drew Collin past the jostling crowd who were eager to buy the precious relics. "We must find a place to live. Then we can come back."

Collin looked back over his shoulder. It would be easy to find Roye again, as long as he had something to sell.

A few blocks away, Tyndale stopped at a three-story house where a woman stood in the doorway. Collin could see a disdainful frown on her face.

"You have not joined the procession today?" William Tyndale asked.

The woman crossed her arms and sniffed. "Ridiculous—as if paying for a relic blessed by the pope is enough to save one's soul."

"Perhaps Martin Luther's ideas suit you better?" Tyndale asked.

"They certainly do. Because of him, the New Testament has been opened to me and many others. But I see you have not joined the crowd either, and I

89

can tell by your accent that you are not a native of Wittenberg."

It did not take much further talk before Tyndale and the housewife came to an understanding about lodgings. In a short time, Collin and Tyndale were at home on the top floor.

"You'll be safe here," the woman said, proud and respectful. "I have strong bolts on my doors."

With living arrangements settled, Collin went back to the market square with William Tyndale. A crowd of people circled Roye. This time, he was shouting protests to two officers.

"These relics are genuine. They have been blessed by the pope himself." He looked around with a wild look. "My partners will tell you so."

The officers shook their heads. "They lodged the complaint themselves before leaving town."

Roye appeared to digest this news. "But I am in holy orders," he said. "I cannot be arrested."

"We know about that, too," an officer said, pulling back Roye's robe. A checkered doublet of green and white showed underneath.

"But I can prove it." Roye was breathing hard. "I know the first verse of the fifty-first psalm.° 'Have mercy upon me, O God, according to thy loving kindness: according unto the multitude of thy tender mercies blot out my transgressions.'"

Collin saw the officers hesitate. "Perhaps we should hand him over to the spiritual courts," one said.

Roye pranced in anguish. "No, no. Set me free.

°If a suspect could quote this verse, it was considered proof that he should either be freed or turned over to church officials.

90

You will bring great trouble to yourselves otherwise."

The officers hesitated. "Do you know anyone who can speak for you?"

Once again Roye looked around wildly. Collin saw Roye's expression change when he discovered William Tyndale.

"Yes—yes. There's a man who can speak for me. He's a famous scholar from England. Save me, Sir William! I am an honest—" Here Roye choked and started again. "I'm a well-deserving friend of yours."

Everyone turned and stared at William Tyndale. It seemed to Collin that every glance stabbed, probed, and questioned. Who was this famous man from England? everyone seemed to be asking. What was he doing in Wittenberg? Collin knew people would discuss the incident. Already the secrecy Tyndale needed so desperately was gone.

Tyndale walked up to the officers and whispered something Collin could not hear. The effect was immediate. With bows and murmurs, the officers handed Roye over to Tyndale. With a final bow, the officers pushed through the crowd and hurried up the street. The onlookers, disappointed, drifted away.

Collin sighed. Tyndale spoke to Roye in a firm voice. "I mentioned Martin Luther's name, and that is why the officers freed you. We won't discuss what you have done. I need someone to help me compare the texts for my Bible translation. If you work with me, I will pay you the salary I promised."

At the mention of money, Roye's eyes gleamed.

"Of course, of course." He shuffled his long feet. "I'll help in every way I can."

o   o   o

In the months that followed, Collin had to admit that Roye was an excellent assistant for Tyndale, but the ex-monk also loved to bring back the news and gossip of the day.

"Did you hear?" he asked one afternoon after returning with a supply of paper. "One of Luther's students was murdered for his heretical views. Only a short time ago he was sitting here at Luther's feet."

Collin listened with uneasy interest. Roye was such a gossip one could never tell when he was telling the truth and when he was exaggerating.

Tyndale did not look up from his manuscript.

"And did you know that Luther's New Testament was denounced as a foul thing and burned?" Roye leaned forward, as if expecting Tyndale to show strong emotion. But Tyndale did not speak.

"And that isn't all." Roye bounced with eagerness. "They do say that certain men are going to put Luther in prison. He'll be kept a kind of free prisoner, and they do say—"

Tyndale clapped both hands to his ears. "Spare me any further news. I want to think only of my translation. It is almost finished."

The day came when Collin saw Tyndale lay his pen down and smile. The New Testament was translated and ready to be printed, but first it must be shown to Martin Luther.

Later, at the roomy cloister where Luther lived, Collin, Tyndale, and Roye were ushered into Luther's study. Luther himself, dressed in a dark professor's gown, greeted them heartily amidst a jumble of books and papers scattered on chairs, tables, and bookcases. Collin sensed the deep emotion both Tyndale and Luther tried to hide when the manuscript of the New Testament in English was laid on the table. For once, Roye remained silent.

Luther fingered the pages with solemn respect. "With the help of God you have accomplished for the English people what God permitted me to do for Germany. Where do you plan to have the New Testament printed—not here in Wittenberg, I hope."

"You don't think it would be wise?" Tyndale asked.

Luther shook his head. "Go to Cologne. Find Peter Quentel. He is an excellent printer." He looked thoughtful. "Have you arranged how to send the printed copies to England?"

The two men looked at each other and burst out laughing. Roye looked indignant. "What other way is there besides smuggling?" he asked. Luther and Tyndale laughed again.

"I shall send them in the accepted way." Tyndale said with a twinkle. "I have merchant friends who will help," he added.

When it was time to go, Luther gave the three his warmest blessing. On the way back to Tyndale's lodgings, Roye walked with a spring in his step, chatting about the money Tyndale would make selling copies of the New Testament.

The landlady must have been watching out the window. She ran out of the house and flung herself on Tyndale. "Hide! Hide! There are men upstairs! They pushed me and threatened me with swords. I don't know what they're doing up there now." She wrung her hands, then pushed all three into the kitchen.

Overhead Collin could hear thumps and grunts. Men were shouting and exclaiming to each other. After a long time, a heavy tramping sounded on the stairs. The front door slammed. Tyndale sprang to his feet, but the landlady would not let him go upstairs until she went out herself to see if the street was clear.

In a few moments she ran back. "The neighbors say there were only two men—one had a red beard. It's strange. I thought there were more, and I didn't even notice the beard."

For a second Tyndale closed his eyes, then without a word raced upstairs. Collin and Roye followed at his heels.

The door to the attic room hung on its hinges. The beds had been ripped apart, the mattresses slashed, and the filling piled into heaps. Books lay helter-skelter. The table was overturned. A chest of drawers gaped open.

Near the window, Collin saw a sticky dark mess. He called Tyndale and Roye to look.

"What's that?" Roye asked, poking gingerly with his foot.

It took a little while to discover that someone had torn out leaves of Luther's New Testament, crumpled them, and poured ink so carefully over the words

94

that none could be read.

Collin made another discovery, an uncrumpled sheet of white paper on which had been scrawled the words, "The English Bible shall burn."

## Chapter 9

## The Forbidden Book

William Tyndale clasped his hands and began to pray. Both Collin and Roye bowed their heads.

"Our Father, we thank Thee this day that Thou hast granted us this blessing," he began.

Collin straightened up in amazement. With wide-open eyes he gazed at Tyndale. What kind of prayer was this? The wreckage of clothing, bedding, and books lay all around them.

"May we accept Thy gift of infinite love and receive all things from Thee, with joy and gratitude," Tyndale went on. Collin closed his eyes again. Tyndale sounded so sincere and warm in his thanks to God that Collin began to doubt his own senses.

After the prayer, Roye burst out with what Collin secretly felt. "How can you thank God for this?" Roye waved his hands. "Have you gone quite out of your mind?"

Tyndale was calm. "Anybody can thank God when things are going well. What merit is there to that? It is when ill fortune comes that we must prove ourselves to God."

Roye grumbled, but Tyndale went on. "Besides,"

he said, pointing to the untouched manuscript of the English New Testament, "God has seen to it that the manuscript was not destroyed."

Collin understood Tyndale's point very well. The English Scriptures were safe.

"Tonight we'll leave for Cologne," Tyndale added. "This deed is warning enough."

The landlady openly wept to see them go. "If I thought your life was safe, I would insist on your staying here," she said. "But I know the church, and I know that if you want your people to have the Scripture, you must go somewhere else. I feel privileged to have known you, sir."

She knelt and would have kissed Tyndale's hand, but he raised her up. "Without the shelter you offered, I could not have completed my translation," he said. "And now I ask your help once more. Tell us where we can find a boat."

The landlady gave directions, and in a short time, Collin, Tyndale, and Roye left Wittenberg and began the long trip to Cologne. It was summer, 1525, just two years since Collin had left Little Sodbury with William Tyndale.

o     o     o

A few days later, Collin followed William Tyndale and Roye down a curved street in Cologne and through a dark doorway just off one of the main streets. It was the first printing shop Collin had ever entered. A curious, pungent smell enveloped him. It bit into his nostrils. Collin sniffed and peered into the dark interior of the shop. Light gleamed through a window high up on one side, and Collin could make out the figures of men seated at sloping tables. The pungent odor was everywhere.

The proprietor of the shop hurried up, rubbing his hands. "I'm Peter Quentel. What can I do for you?"

"I have a work here to be printed in English. Can this be done?"

"Of course."

"Is your work kept confidential?" Tyndale asked.

Peter Quentel bowed. "Of course. No one in my shop talks about a customer's private affairs. Now, what do you wish to have us print?"

Tyndale handed over the manuscript. Peter Quentel looked through it, raised his eyebrows, but made no comment. "How many copies will you want?" he asked.

"Six thousand—no, make it three to start with," Tyndale said.

Peter Quentel glanced up quickly, "You fear seizure, perhaps?"

Tyndale nodded.

"Very well," Peter Quentel said. "I suggest a quarto edition, with prologue, marginal references, and annotations."

To Collin these words might as well have been in Greek, but William Tyndale beamed satisfaction.

"You're sure you want annotations, and not just the straight Scriptures?" Peter Quentel asked.

"Yes," Tyndale answered with conviction. "Without my explanations, people might not understand the Scriptures."

"Just as you say." Peter Quentel made an entry

on a ledger. "Now I'm sure you would like to see my shop."

Collin could see better now, and in more detail. Men sat on benches before slanted wooden trays divided into boxes. Above each tray, at eye level, a stick held a sheet of paper which each man studied, reaching into one compartment after another for tiny slivers of wood tipped with metal. Collin soon discovered each tray held letters. The largest tray, which was next to the man forming words, was full of *e*'s. "Because *e* is the most used letter," the man explained.

A boy no older than Collin, wearing a big apron, tacked up wet sheets of paper, or hung them over a line. To Collin every action in the shop was mysterious and fascinating.

Peter Quentel handed the New Testament manuscript to a plump man whose cap hung over one ear. He ran a calloused thumb through the pages and placed the first sheet on the stick in front of him. He began to reach into one case after the other, never taking his eyes off the handwritten page.

"That's Hubert," Peter Quentel explained in an aside. "He's my best printer. Been with us for years."

Collin stayed to watch. Hubert put letter after letter together in a little groove. Sometimes he put a bit of wood between letters. Slowly Collin began to understand how words were separated. He tried to read the metal letters, but to his alarm, he could not make out a single word. He started after William Tyndale to warn him that the printing would not be in English. As he moved, he knocked against a wooden case and a whole tray of type fell on the floor.

a buzz of mocking laughter rose from the other printers. Hubert hissed an angry word at Collin and began
picking up the type. Collin, his face hot, bent to help.

"Just leave the type alone," Hubert said in a
sharp voice, sorting over a handful of metal-tipped
type. "You've caused enough trouble for one day."

Collin stammered an apology. "What language is
that?" he asked timidly.

"English," Hubert snapped. "What does it matter
to you? You can't read it anyway."

"Yes, I can, but these letters look different."

Hubert threw back his head and laughed. "He
can't read type," he called to the others. There was
a general laugh.

Tears smarted in Collin's eyes. He moved toward
the apprentice, who sat on a high stool watching.
When Collin came close, the other boy turned to his
case and with great care set a stick full of type in
a long tray.

"Are you going to work here?" the apprentice asked without looking up.

Collin sensed the hostility in the other boy. "Why,
no. I'm just here to help my master."

"Well, you'd better not try to weasel in on my
job."

"I won't. You have to know a lot to do that work."
The admiration in Collin's voice must have touched
the other boy.

"It isn't hard once you catch on," he said with
pride. "You have to learn to read words backward."

"Backward? But why?" Collin asked.

"Because when you ink the letters and stamp it
on paper, the print comes out so you can read it."

100

Collin was delighted. "So that's the mystery of printing!" Soon he was spending most of his days in the printing shop, while Tyndale and Roye, in nearby lodgings, began translating the Old Testament.

Collin ran errands for the printers and cleaned up the trimmings of wood and metal scattered on the floor. The apprentice let him reach for type, and Collin learned how to spell words backward. When someone spilled a tray—an accident that was not uncommon, Collin found out—he put the type back. The men joked at his eagerness to help, but Collin did not mind.

Letter by letter, line by line, Hubert set up the New Testament. Sometimes he had to scrape or file a letter, or insert thin wedges of wood in order to space out a line. Whenever Collin heard the words, "Justify the lines," he knew another four pages, or quarto sheet, of the New Testament would be placed in the big wooden frame, the type surface smoothed, inked with a dauber of sheepskin stuffed with wool, and the heavy press screwed down on thick, porous paper dampened overnight.

One day the apprentice beckoned to Collin. "Hubert says something terrible has happened to the type."

Collin hurried to Hubert's side. Other printers, with solemn worried faces, left their stools and crowded around Collin.

"What's happened?" Collin asked.

Hubert shook his head. "We can't go on. There's a type louse loose in the form."

"A what?" Collin asked, bewildered.

"A type louse. You know what a regular louse is, don't you?"

"Yes. I've seen lots of them."

"Well, there's a special kind of louse that eats only type. This one's been eating up the New Testament as fast as I can set it up. Do you want to see if you can find it?"

Collin trembled in eagerness. "Oh, yes. Maybe I can catch it. I'm not afraid."

There was an undercurrent of coughs and clearing of throats.

Hubert bent solemnly over a square wooden form where handfuls of type had been removed. Water lay in small pools between the type columns.

Hubert pointed. "There it is—right there at the bottom. I saw it move."

Collin bent to look at the strange insect. Hubert shoved up a column of type, forcing the water to rise like a fountain in Collin's face. At first he did not understand what had happened and tried to mop the slimy water off his face. A roar of laughter exploded all around the composing room. Typesetters pounded their composing sticks on the frames and laughed. Collin was weak with relief that nothing was harming Sir William's New Testament. He laughed too, and a murmur of approval ran around the room.

"You've graduated with honors, my boy," Hubert said. "Each of us has been initiated into the printing guild by means of the type louse. You may be sure we'll not let any louse destroy the English Scriptures, will we, men?"

"Destroy *what*?" A deep, startled voice in front of the shop made everyone turn. A small man Collin had never seen before stood watching the printers. "What an odd place to find—" He broke off the

102

words and continued blandly, "To find something being printed in English here in Germany."

Somehow, Collin knew the man meant to say, "What an odd place to find the English Scriptures." Collin's whole body tingled with the sense of danger. Who was this man who carried himself like a pouter pigeon? Why was he here, and what would he do about the printing of the Scriptures in English?

The man was small, like Tyndale, but with a round face and uptilted nose that seemed shaped to sniff out secrets.

Peter Quentel approached him. "What can I do for you?"

"My name is—well, call me John Cochlaeus. I was dean of the church in Frankfurt."

"Ah, yes," Peter Quentel murmured. "There was a little uprising there recently, was there not?"

Cochlaeus reddened. "Never mind that. I've come to see you about printing some works of a twelfth-century abbot. Perhaps you don't remember Rupert of Deutz?" As he spoke, Cochlaeus darted quick glances about the shop. Collin kept his face turned away so that he would not call attention to himself, but he listened without shame. The safety of the English New Testament might well be at stake if he did not know what the man was after.

"Do you wish these works printed in German?" Peter Quentel asked.

Cochlaeus stared. "Of course. What other language is there—other than Latin?" He laughed and Peter Quentel joined in halfheartedly. "Rupert has a message for our day," Cochlaeus went on. "He said, 'To be ignorant of Scripture is to be ignorant of Christ.'"

Collin's tense muscles relaxed. The abbot's words might have been Tyndale's own statement. The message of the twelfth-century abbot was certainly not the church's viewpoint. Collin looked at John Cochlaeus with friendly interest.

Cochlaeus chatted on. "You see, the heretic Osiander of Nuremberg is in treaty with the present abbot of Deutz to publish Rupert's writings. I begged the abbot to entrust the manuscripts of his celebrated predecessor to me. I will undertake to print them at my own expense and prove that he belongs to the church."

Collin's mind whirled. What a hateful little man this Cochlaeus was! How could the printers work on the English Scriptures and the church publication without Tyndale's secret becoming known?

Tyndale was alarmed at the news, Collin saw later. Every day, early in the morning, Tyndale and Roye arrived at the printing shop to check over the previous day's output, leaving before other customers came in. Every day John Cochlaeus dropped in, too, and Collin watched his every move.

The printed quarto pages multiplied. Collin never tired of seeing the imprinting of four pages at a time by the heavy screw press. It seemed to him that every sheet was a victory over the powers of darkness. He understood more than ever before how God guided Tyndale. The little man never seemed to tire. He ate only when Collin pushed food under his nose. Tyndale's energy seemed to fire the restless Roye, so that he too seemed a tireless helper.

The strain of constant alertness at the printing shop tired Collin. One evening he fell asleep be-

104

*Peter Quentel begins printing Tyndale's New Testament.*

hind the printing press and woke to the sound of drunken laughter.

"Here's a thank-you, sir, for this fine drink. It sets well after a long day," he heard Hubert tell someone.

"It takes away the smell of ink, indeed," a second man said.

Collin recognized the voice of an experienced printer who had just recently come from another city to work for Peter Quentel. Collin peered around the press. In flickering candlelight he watched the two printers wave tankards of liquor high in the air. A third man, Cochlaeus himself, sat on a stool, not drinking, but refilling the men's tankards from a crock.

"I hear there is an Englishman who is having printing done in this shop," Cochlaeus said in friendly tones.

"Aye, that there be, a tall cantankerous man with bad jokes and worse poems." Hubert raised his tankard, gulped, and smacked his lips.

Collin mentally applauded Hubert's cleverness in not betraying William Tyndale.

"We're making history, right here in this shop." The new printer thumped his tankard down so hard that the liquid sloshed over the side. He licked it off and took a long drink.

"Making history?" Cochlaeus moved his stool to the counter and leaned back on his elbow.

"Yes, sir, and I say whether England's King Henry and his Cardinal Wolsey like it or not, all the English will shortly become Lutheran."

Hubert put a finger to his lips and shook his head. 106

Cochlaeus leaned forward. "What makes you say that?"

"Why, sir," the new printer said, "we're printing the New Testament in English in this shop. It'll change the world, won't it, Hubert?"

To Collin's horror, Hubert nodded.

Cochlaeus hummed. "So you have an English Luther here, eh? Doesn't he know Cologne is strongly opposed to such heresy?"

The new printer winked. "Well, sir, everybody wants to buy forbidden books. Like forbidden fruit, they're sweeter."

Hubert gave a drunken guffaw. "That's right. The two Englishmen seem to think so, anyway."

Cochlaeus jumped off the stool. "Two Englishmen? I thought there was only one. Who is this other man?"

Collin clenched his fists and waited for Hubert to betray William Tyndale. What sickened him more was the wink Cochlaeus gave to the new printer. He knew then that the new man had been planted as a spy.

Chapter **10**

## *Daring Journey*

In a shrill, urgent voice, Cochlaeus asked again, "Who is the other man?"

Collin watched from his hiding place. Hubert plunked his tankard on the counter. "His name? I don't quite remember."

Cochlaeus filled Hubert's tankard from his crock. "Where could I find him? It's very important."

Hubert dropped his head on his arms. His hand dropped away from the tankard. Cochlaeus grunted in annoyance, gave Hubert a shake, then turned to the new printer. Collin watched Cochlaeus pass a coin to the man, who eyed it, bit it, and put it in his pocket.

"All right, what else did you find out?" Cochlaeus asked.

"All I know is that the Englishman—or rather, the two of them, which I didn't know—they're here before daybreak and sometimes after dark. What they do in the middle of the day I know not. You must indeed be an early riser to catch them."

"Let me see these quarto sheets." Cochlaeus moved toward the composing room.

Hubert sat up, his body tense. "No one is allowed back there."

"Well, then, just tell me how many copies of the New Testament you're printing."

"Three thousand," Hubert said.

Cochlaeus sucked in his breath. "And where does the money come from for all this?"

"Why, sir, the English merchants." Hubert slumped over again. His noisy breathing filled the shop.

For one fear-split second, Collin thought Cochlaeus was coming into the composing section, but the little snub-nosed man hesitated and then left the shop, followed by the new printer.

Collin waited a few minutes before running home to tell Tyndale what had happened. The next day Roye left to find out what he could about Cochlaeus. For several days he came back without news. One afternoon he flung himself into the room, his step jaunty, and a wide grin showing all his teeth.

"I've found out all about Cochlaeus," he said, and began to chant:

"A little, praty, foolish poade,
    And though his stature be quite small
    I've heard men say he lacks no gall,
    More venomous than any toad."

Tyndale frowned and laid down his pen.

"I have news—such news!" Roye capered about the room. "Cochlaeus has told Herman Rincke—he's an important senator here in Cologne—all about the English New Testament. Rincke didn't believe it at first, but he planted a spy in the shop—"

Collin grunted. This time, for once, he had been right about the spy.

109

Tyndale jumped up. "The church sets it spies on me in earnest—ravening wolves, robbing the soul of man of the bread of life. Yet God will not abandon me. Is it not His own Word that is imperiled? We must leave Cologne. We'll gather up what has been printed and leave secretly tonight."

At the printing shop, there was a strange quiet. The men huddled together in the composing room, talking in low tones. Peter Quentel greeted Tyndale with such a subdued air that Collin knew something was dreadfully wrong.

"Gentlemen, I regret that an order came from the Senate this very afternoon to stop printing the English New Testament."

"It was to be expected," William Tyndale said. "I will pay what I owe you and take the quarto sheets that have been printed and go to some other city."

The printers looked at each other.

"I appreciate your sympathetic interest," Tyndale said. "I am not dismayed. God is with me on this undertaking. If you will be so good as to bind the sheets together so that we can carry them, we will leave right away so that the shop will not be under suspicion."

No one moved. The quietness became oppressive.

"I do not know how to tell you—" Peter Quentel began. "You see, when the officers brought the orders, they—" He stopped and looked away.

"They confiscated the printed sheets," Tyndale finished.

Collin felt a sickening hollowness. This news meant that all the work of printing would have to be begun again. He looked at William Tyndale. How could he face such discouragement? But Tyndale stood with eyes closed, his face calm, almost serene. Collin felt ashamed of his own despair. What right had he to feel anything except the courage Tyndale showed at every misfortune?

Peter Quentel went on. "There was nothing I could do. Resistance would mean closing the shop and putting all these men out of work."

Tyndale took out his money bag. "I quite understand. You did the only possible thing under the circumstances. Kindly let me know what I owe you."

When the bill was settled, Collin followed Tyndale and Roye out of the shop. It was almost dusk. Collin heard running footsteps and turned. The apprentice ran up to him, holding something under his work apron. "Here," he said, holding out some printed sheets. "I saved these. There are ten quarto sheets— that's all I could manage. Don't tell anyone at the shop about this, will you? I hope your master finds someplace to get his New Testament printed." The apprentice waved good-bye and hurried away.

Collin showed Tyndale the quarto sheets. Tyndale's look of radiant gratitude brought a lump to Collin's throat.

"Not all is lost," Tyndale said. "But how are we going to leave Cologne? The city gates will be watched. The hot breath of the church is at our very heels."

The question was a serious one. Back at their lodgings, Collin started to pack. Roye stood at the window looking at the street below. He began to chuckle. Collin, indignant at Roye's lack of seriousness, ran to see what had amused the ex-monk. Below, a group of boys seized one of their companions. With shouts of laughter the others clipped the boy's hair into a monk's tonsure. The boy laughed with the others, folded his arms, and walked with slow steps, imitating a monk. The group moved down the street, laughing and talking.

"What are they doing?" Collin asked.

Roye whirled around and clapped his hands. "It means there's a church procession today. It means there's a way we can leave the city under the officials' very noses."

Collin was certain Roye had lost his senses. Tyndale did not even reply to Roye's remarks.

"But don't you see?" Roye asked. "We'll become part of the procession and march right out of the city gates. Leave everything to me." He slipped on his monk's robe. "Wait here."

Later Roye returned with several bundles under his arm. "Don't ask me any questions about where I got these. Needless to say, I haven't been a monk without learning a thing or two." He pulled out a choir boy's robe, a long brown gown, and a pair of scissors. "You first, my boy," he said to Collin.

In a few minutes Collin ran his fingers over the band of hair circling his head.

Roye stood back and eyed his handiwork. "Not that boys your age usually have a tonsure, but people will realize it was a boyish prank played on you by some of your friends, just like those boys this afternoon. It's quite a usual thing before a procession." Roye waved his scissors over Tyndale's head. "Now you, sir."

112

Tyndale hesitated.

Roye looked offended. "You said yourself that all the city gates will be watched. Do you want that toad of a Cochlaeus to throw you in prison? Did I tell you what Senator Rincke told the Senate?" Roye waved the scissors again. " 'Seize the heretic who troubles England as Luther troubled Germany.' "

With an exclamation, Tyndale peeled off his tight black cap. In a short time, he too had a circle of hair like a monk's.

"Now it's my turn." Roye handed the scissors to Tyndale, who hesitated once more.

"I've never cut hair," he said.

"Do you want the New Testament in the hands of Englishmen?" Roye reminded him. "I forgot to tell you that Cochlaeus is writing to King Henry and to Cardinal Wolsey about your work."

Tyndale began snipping off Roye's hair in a circular band. When he was through, he stepped back just as Roye had done to him. "It's a little one-sided," he said. "Your halo has slipped a little." He laid the scissors down. "What next?"

Roye taught Tyndale and Collin how to walk without body motion. He placed the ball of his foot on the floor and let his heel settle into place. The three marched around and around while Roye chanted Latin.

Next, Roye opened one of the bundles and brought out a satin pillow and carved wooden box. Tyndale's handwritten manuscript of the New Testament fit into it. Roye fastened the box with pillow cords. "Now, when you put on your robes, we will wait until the church procession passes the house. Then we will slip into line and keep marching past the cathedral and out the city gates. I'll think up some good reason by that time to tell the guards."

Tyndale agreed that the plan, although daring, was good. He began to pile up his books ready to take.

"You can't carry those," Roye said. "The only belongings any of us can take are what we can wear under the robes. That's a great deal. I know. I've had lots of practice."

Collin and Tyndale put on all the clothes they could. Collin remembered the quarto sheets. "What about these?" he asked.

The three stared at one another. There was no more room in the wooden box. The quarto sheets could not be carried by hand.

"Wrap them around me," Collin suggested. Tyndale and Roye placed the quarto sheets around Collin's waist and bound them with cord. Collin moved stiffly, his arms held out at his sides. He could not bend or sit.

Roye handed him a wax taper. "Here. You must carry this when we go outside."

"Where are we going when we leave Cologne?" Collin asked.

"We'll go to Worms," Tyndale said. "Quentel mentioned a printer there—Peter Schoeffer. He is a son of an associate of Gutenberg. I wonder if Gutenberg had as much trouble with his Bible as I'm having."

Roye started to reply but stopped. Chanting sounded far down the street. The three tiptoed down the stairs, dressed in robes. Tyndale left money and a note on the table for the landlady.

Outside, Collin felt tense and yet curiously light-headed, as if he walked in a dream. The quarto sheets pricked him if he moved too quickly. He could hear the church procession coming closer. Chanting swelled and diminished. Then he saw the banners of satin, embroidered with gold thread. One man carried a huge wooden cross. Other men carried relics on satin pillows. Still others held tapers high.

Townspeople walked at a respectful distance behind the relic bearers. Roye lit Collin's taper and gave him a nudge. "Fall into line," he whispered.

Collin stepped into the line of procession, with Tyndale right behind bearing the boxed manuscript of the English New Testament on the satin pillow. Collin held his taper in front of him and tried to remember to walk in the easy, flowing ripple of the churchmen ahead of him.

He was just beginning to feel at ease when from one of the houses lining the street a child called from an open doorway to someone in the group of people behind Collin.

"Mother! There's Mother!" The child ran into the street with open arms.

Collin heard a woman behind him call out, "No, no, Hans. You must go back to the house."

There was a flurry of movement. Collin guessed that the mother had given her child a push. Then Tyndale exclaimed, and the next instant the wooden box sailed past Collin's face and crashed on the cobbled street. The leaves of Tyndale's English Scriptures scattered in all directions for everyone to see.

## Chapter 11

## The Hidden Word

Helpless, unable to bend, Collin stood stiff as a bell. The handwritten sheets of the New Testament lay strewn of the cobblestones all around him. Collin tightened his grip on the taper, determined to jab the flame into any curious onlooker who stepped too close. To his surprise, no one tried. Instead, everyone drew back in round-eyed awe.

Roye grabbed Collin's taper and waved it. "This is the devil's deed, but by this sacred flame, the Word of God will be kept intact."

Roye lowered the taper and passed it lengthwise and crosswise over the scattered sheets. William Tyndale scooped them up. When the manuscript was back in the box, Collin tried to catch up with the procession ahead. It disappeared around a curve in the street. Roye ran up and whispered, "Drop out at the next church. Tyndale will follow you, and I'll lead the townspeople to the cathedral and then come back. Wait for me."

Collin turned in at the entrance of a small church. Tyndale came right behind, breathing out a vast sigh. Not long after, Roye appeared, jubilant that his

116

*Tyndale, Collin, and Roye leave Cologne under disguise.*

plan was working so well. At the city gates, Roye, with many gestures, explained to the guards that the wooden box had been cursed and would have to be buried in unconsecrated ground. The guards jumped to open the gates and stood back from the box as if it had been filled with a deadly poison.

Once out of sight, Collin, Tyndale, and Roye took off their robes. Tyndale unbound the quarto sheets from around Collin's waist and rolled them like a scroll. The three walked by the river until they came to a landing place where they boarded a river boat.

The trip on the Rhine River took several days. Collin gazed at the blur of high hills, topped by castles, and marveled at the vineyards on the steep slopes. Strong currents tugged at the boat, almost dashing it at times against crags. The trip was like Tyndale's own life, Collin reflected. There were cross currents and perils at every turn, but the pilot of the boat was skillful. It soothed Collin to think God Himself was Tyndale's pilot.

At Worms, they had no trouble finding lodging and food markets. Tyndale soon met merchants who wanted to help send copies of the New Testament to England as soon as the book was printed. They did not use the word *smuggle*, but laughed and winked at each other.

Collin was delighted to see William Tyndale so elated. Even Roye's new restlessness did not seem to bother Tyndale. Roye did not even go to the printing shop at first but spent his time roaming the streets.

At the shop, Peter Schoeffer, the manager, treated Tyndale with respect. He listened to Tyndale's request and thumbed through the pages with care.

"I'm afraid my men can't complete this."

For the first time Collin could remember, William Tyndale seemed to stagger under the blow. Collin inwardly raged. Didn't God want His Word to be printed so that His people could read it? Why was there always trouble?

Tyndale handed his handwritten copy to Peter Schoeffer. "I have the complete New Testament here. Won't your printers be able to follow English?"

The humbleness of his tone made Collin ashamed of his anger.

"That isn't the problem," Peter Schoeffer was saying. "You see, we don't have this kind of font. We have our own kind of type, exclusive with us. To mix types would produce a very uneven effect. I would never put our watermark on a single page of inferior work."

Tyndale looked questioning.

Peter Schoeffer jutted out his chin. "You know, don't you, that my father was the first man after Gutenberg to print a complete Bible? That was back in 1462. The name Schoeffer will never be sullied by less than perfect printing."

"But I must complete this." Tyndale's slender face was earnest. "You were highly recommended. Do I understand that you refuse to print the New Testament?"

Peter Schoeffer raised his hands in protest. "Not at all, not at all. You completely misunderstand me. I mean that it would be better to start over, so that your copies will have uniform print. Furthermore, I question putting in all this prologue and explanations of the text. The Bible stands alone, my father always said."

Collin could see Tyndale hesitate, and he knew the question Tyndale was asking himself. *Would there be enough money to start over?*

After a moment, Tyndale agreed to Peter Schoeffer's suggestion. "How soon can it be printed?"

Peter Schoeffer considered. "You have just the New Testament here, do you not?"

"Yes. I'm translating the Old Testament now, but it won't be ready for a long time."

Collin watched Peter Schoeffer jot down a few figures. "It will take three to four months," he said. "I'll put two shifts of printers on it."

Once again Collin spent most of his days in the printing shop. The men welcomed his help and showed surprise at how well Collin knew certain passages. When they asked him to recite, Collin usually quoted his favorite passage:

"O oure father, which art in heven halowed be
thy name. Let thy kyngdom come. Thy wyll be
fulfilled, as well in erth, as hit ys in heven.
Geve vs this daye our dayly breade. And forgeve
vs oure treaspases, even as we forgeve them whych
treaspas vs. Lede vs nott in to temptacion,
but delyvre vs from yvell, Amen." °

Once again the printed pages were piling up, this time in octavo, eight pages at a time. True to his promise, Peter Schoeffer had two shifts of printers at work on the New Testament. There were no suspicious people visiting the shop, as far as Collin could see. The only worry there could possibly be was the shortage of money. Roye wore a long face these days

° F. F. Bruce, *The English Bible*, Oxford University Press, New York, 1961 p. 35.

and spoke in sulky tones.

Still, Collin felt lighthearted one night when he started home from the shop. Even heavy footsteps on the cobblestones behind him did not stop his humming to himself, but he quickened his steps. The footsteps behind him quickened, too.

All his senses alert, now, Collin began to run.

"There's his boy. Don't let him get away," a man called out.

The voice sounded familiar. Collin looked over his shoulder. Even in the dusk there was no mistaking the fiery red beard of John Tisen, Tyndale's former student and avowed enemy. Another man was with him.

With pulses leaping, Collin sprinted down the street, looking for an open doorway. With a desperate look around, he darted down a narrow alley. With horrible realization, he saw he had entered a dead-end court. A wall twice his height loomed ahead of him. Collin crouched and sprang. His fingers clawed the stone wall, missing the top by several feet. Collin whirled, facing the men, with his back to the wall. John Tisen rushed toward him with a walking staff upraised.

"Where is William Tyndale?"

"I don't know, sir."

John Tisen grunted in scorn. "Tell the truth, or it will go hard with you."

Blood pounded in Collin's ears. He couldn't seem to think but he managed to ask, "Did you want to see him?"

The second man laughed. "Yes, we do, and the King of England and Cardinal Wolsey would like to see him too. Where is he?"

121

Collin was beginning to catch his breath. "He goes out to see the sick and the poor many times. I couldn't say where he is."

John Tisen shook Collin, but the other man pulled him off. "Let the boy alone. It's Tyndale we want. You can tell your master we'll pursue him to the ends of the earth. Isn't that what you said, John?"

John Tisen snarled a reply, but turned away, flinging Collin against the wall. After they left, a woman ran out of the side door of a house next to the court.

"What did those men want?" she asked. "I saw them from upstairs. Did they hurt you?"

Her sympathetic tone led Collin to tell more than he meant to.

"It's clear that your Sir William will have to go in hiding. Have him come here," the woman said. "I have Luther's New Testament, and I shall be proud to help the English Luther."

That night, Collin brought Tyndale and Roye to the new lodgings. Tyndale had simply sighed on hearing Collin's story and had begun packing at once.

The next evening Roye came home early. "Sir William, someone wants to see you."

William Tyndale gave a short laugh. "I think many men would like to see me—starting with the King of England and his cardinal."

Roye was insistent. "But this man has an important message from the English merchants."

"Did the man have a red beard?" Collin asked.

"No, he did not have a red beard. His name I know not, but if it be your pleasure, Sir William,

122

to go where he is, he is exceedingly desirous to speak with you."

Tyndale shook his head. "I am not interested," he said curtly.

"But the messenger says he has a business offer that means money."

Roye could never mention the word *money* without a greedy look. Collin tried to remember how long it had been since Roye had been paid.

"The money *is* getting low," Tyndale admitted.

Roye kept on urging. "I've worked hard all these months, and you've given me barely enough to exist on."

"You shall be paid," Tyndale promised. "You may tell this messenger I'll see him in the open field past the south gate of the city tomorrow at dusk. Tell him to arrive alone. If anyone is with him, I will not show myself."

Collin spent a restless night. Was Tyndale going to be trapped tomorrow? Tyndale, too, appeared uneasy all the next day.

"Let me go first," Collin pleaded when they arrived at the city gates. "They won't hurt me." He ran on ahead.

In a few moments a man came into the field. He looked disappointed when he saw Collin.

"Where is Sir William?" he asked. "Wouldn't he come?"

"He wants to be sure you are alone."

"I understand," the messenger said. "You can see that I am by myself."

William Tyndale walked slowly over the field and greeted the messenger. "Do you know me?" he asked.

"I do not well remember you," the messenger said, "but if you are William Tyndale, fortunate be our meeting. I have found you a merchant who with ready money will buy a thousand copies of the New Testament."

Collin gasped with excitement.

Tyndale smiled. "That is good news indeed. Without the aid of the English merchants, I could not have completed my work. Who is helping me now?"

The messenger looked embarrassed. "It is my lord the Bishop of London."

Tyndale's astonishment lasted only a minute. Then he burst into laughter. This time it was the messenger's turn to look astonished.

"Here is the money," he said, pulling out a money sack.

Tyndale laughed again. "I see through this scheme. The Bishop of London wants my New Testaments so that he can burn them up. But I am glad, and I shall accept his offer, for two benefits will come out of this. I shall have the money to pay my debts and the world will cry out against the burning of God's Word." Tyndale accepted the sack of money and bade the messenger good-bye.

The succeeding weeks went by swiftly. By December, 1525, six thousand copies of the New Testament had been printed. William Tyndale sent letters to his friends in England warning them to be on the watch for the first smuggled copies. First of all, he arranged to have the Bishop of London's copies delivered. When it was time to tuck the other copies into bales of cloth or flour, Collin helped mark an inconspicuous cross on the ones containing the New Testament.

The first ship was almost ready to sail. Tyndale paced the dock, his gaze never leaving the ship. Collin sensed Tyndale's torment and uncertainty. How could anyone be sure of the fate of the English Scriptures?

In a flash of insight, Collin knew what had to be done. "Sir William, let me go to England and help distribute the New Testaments."

Tyndale stopped his pacing. He smiled and put his hands on Collin's shoulders. "You have been with me these three years. You have lived all the risks I have. You are young, strong, and brave, but a mere boy cannot outwit Cardinal Wolsey's spies. No, this work is for men of the world."

But Collin would not give up. "I know the secret sign on the bales. I could help your brother unpack them. I could be a lot of help; really, I could."

At last Tyndale consented. When the ship sailed, Collin was on it. All the way to England he planned how he could help distribute the thousands of copies of the New Testament. Paul Blake would help, he knew. In the last three years, Paul must have learned to know every corner in London and every person who could be trusted. Collin almost hugged himself remembering the secret whistle code Paul's friends used to warn each other of important news.

With his head full of dreams and plans, Collin could hardly wait until the ship landed at the wharf on the Thames River. He flung himself past bales and barrels on the dockside and hurried to John Tyndale's warehouse. He rattled the door of the office in his impatience and slipped inside. A clerk on a high stool turned from a big ledger, completely indifferent. "Yes?"

Dashed by the cool reception, Collin gulped and tried to speak calmly. "Is John Tyndale here?"

"He'll be back presently. He's watching for an important shipment he's expecting." The clerk scratched his head with a quill pen and turned back to his accounts.

"I'll wait for him. This is important, too."

The clerk looked over his shoulder. "Are you from the continent?" he asked with a little more interest.

"I just came from there."

The clerk leaped down and started for the door. "Please excuse me. I'll find Mr. Tyndale at once. Do be seated. He'll be right here."

In a few minutes John Tyndale hurried in. His expression was restrained and cautious. "You came with the—the shipment?" He did not seem to recognize Collin.

"Yes. Sir William didn't have time to write. It was decided on so quickly."

John Tyndale relaxed a little.

"I'm Collin Hartley. I went with Sir William from here three years ago."

This time John Tyndale beamed. "But you've grown so much I didn't know you."

Collin heard and appreciated the respect in John Tyndale's voice. It was as if Sir William's brother accepted him as an adult, and he felt a grateful pride. After all, three years with William Tyndale would help anyone grow up.

John Tyndale cautioned Collin. "We'll keep this shipment as secret as possible. Do you know which are the marked bundles?"

"Yes."

"Stay with me, then. The less the dock workers know when they're unloading, the safer we'll all be."

The rest of the day Collin pointed out the marked bales. John Tyndale ordered them piled to one side. When the dock workers left for the day, Collin and John Tyndale undid the bales one by one, probing for the copies of the New Testament and carrying them inside the warehouse to a specially prepared niche. John Tyndale stayed to arrange them, and Collin went out for more.

An excited voice behind a pile of goods stopped him short.

"I tell you, I saw them—saw them with my own eyes. Loaded in those fardels, they were."

The rough voice indicated a dock worker.

"Yes, yes, but what did you see?" an impatient voice asked.

"Why, books by the thousands," the worker said.

"Ah, that should make a fine bonfire at St. Paul's cross," the other man replied. "Show me to the place."

Collin heard the words in shocked disbelief. Were the New Testaments to be confiscated and burned before a single copy could be sold?

Chapter **12**

## *Glorious Exile*

Collin's first thought was to warn John Tyndale that the shipment of New Testaments had been discovered. He dodged among the bales and darted toward the warehouse. A shout behind him spurred him on. In his hurry, he tripped on a loose rope end and sprawled on the damp planking of the wharf. Before he could move, he felt himself pulled up. A young man with a serious, scholarly face, brushed Collin off.

"Are you hurt?" the young man asked.

Collin shook his head.

"Then could you tell me where John Tyndale's warehouse is?"

Even the young man's knowledge of the name did not quiet Collin's suspicions. No one could be trusted now.

John Tyndale ran out from the office. "What is the matter here?"

"My name is Robert Necton," the young man said. "I would like to buy a few of the books you have just received."

"What books do you mean?"

The young man grew more assured. "It is my understanding that God's Word in the English language is now among us. I know the risk, and I accept the responsibility."

"Come back tomorrow," John Tyndale said.

Robert Necton bowed and left.

Collin watched the young man until he was out of sight.

"Well, what do you think?" John Tyndale asked. "Shall we trust him? We have to make a start someplace."

"Why don't you let me find my friend Paul Blake?" Collin explained Paul's system of communicating with his friends. "He knows people, and if he doesn't, his friends do. But I just know he could tell whether to trust a person or not."

John Tyndale reflected. "We certainly don't want the shipment seized by Cardinal Wolsey's agents. Go find your friend. He sounds as if he could be a great help."

It was no surprise to Collin to find Paul in his accustomed place in front of St. Paul's Cathedral. Except for Paul's new height, it might have been three days instead of three years since Collin saw him. Paul whooped with delight at the challenge of distributing the New Testaments under the very eyes of Cardinal Wolsey's spies.

At the wharf, when Robert Necton came, Paul nodded his approval. John Tyndale brought out both bound and unbound copies of the New Testament. Robert Necton took both kinds, paying three shillings two pence apiece for the bound copies, and less for the unbound.

"I'll send you another man you can trust. George Constantine is his name," he said when he left.

From that time on, Collin heard more names and brought out more copies of the New Testament than he thought possible. Through a leather seller named Tewkesbury, a grocer named John Petit, John Tyball of Steeple Bumstead, John Pykas of Colchester, Thomas Hilles, Robert Barnes, the New Testaments flowed out like a river. The curate of All-Hallows Church, Thomas Garret, offered his house to store copies. Other copies were hidden in warehouses at the Steleyard.

Collin helped Paul organize his friends, from the apple woman to the handler of horses. Each one kept a few copies of the New Testament in basket or sack.

Collin wrote to William Tyndale, sending the letter by a messenger John Tyndale hired. In the letter Collin listed some of the people who bought the New Testament. There were apprentices, tailors, founders, saddlers, weavers, bricklayers, fishmongers, servants who had bought copies from Paul's friends. John Tyndale listed scholars, monks, and priests.

The letter had hardly gone when Paul brought bad news. A man had been caught with copies of the New Testament in his possession. The punishment was to be public. Paul and Collin went to the market place to watch. The king's officials set the man backwards on a horse and tacked copies of the New Testament to his cloak. They led the horse through streets thronged with people. At St. Paul's churchyard a bonfire had been made. With a whip at his back, the man unfastened each copy of the New Testament and threw it into the fire.

Spectators murmured to each other. "They say these New Testaments are overrunning the country," one said.

"This man Tyndale poisons the land with his horrible heresies. He is Antichrist himself," another exclaimed.

Collin could not bear to listen to any more remarks. He and Paul left. Paul was cheerful. "Don't worry. The church can't possibly get hold of every copy. The word will soon be all over England, and people will demand copies."

At the warehouse, when Collin and Paul brought out armloads of New Testaments from the secret hiding place ready to be sold, it seemed to Collin that the books made an invisible chain from one hand to another. Every day the boys delivered copies to Paul's friends to sell on the street, in market stalls, and from under the tables in their homes.

Coming back from one errand, they learned from John Tyndale that the king's officials had visited a number of merchants at the Steleyard.

"Eight or ten took the oath," he said.

For a moment Collin did not understand. "What oath?"

"Why, they had to swear they had nothing to do with heretical books, but they will have to appear before Cardinal Wolsey to answer charges, just the same." He looked worried. "I wonder if we'll be next."

For several weeks, there was no further word. Then Paul brought more news from his friends. "The bishops met and passed a law to burn all untrue translations of the Scriptures. The Bishop

131

of London is in charge."

The next news came soon. The Bishop of London had ferreted out hundreds of copies of the New Testament and set the date for their burning in October, 1526.

"One of the sellers recanted," Paul reported. "They gave him his choice—to recant or be burned at the stake."

The terrifying words plumbed deep into Collin. Would William Tyndale one day be faced with such a choice? He put the thought out of his mind, comforting himself that William Tyndale would never return to England. His self-chosen exile was his only protection, so long as he kept hidden.

On the day of the burning, Collin and Paul hurried through the narrow streets to St. Paul's cross, the crucifix by the great north door of the cathedral. A high scaffold had been erected. A close-knit pile of fagots lay ready. Crowds of people gaped and exclaimed.

Two clergymen near Collin and Paul watched the preparations. "I say burn the heretics themselves, not their books," one said.

The other agreed. "Stop the breeding at the source."

On the other side of Collin a man spoke to his neighbor. "Is this Luther's New Testament?"

"Oh, no," his neighbor replied. "This is a translation of the Scriptures by one of England's own men. Cursed be his name and cursed be his heresy for putting the New Testament into our own language."

"Our own language?" There was such a note of hope in the man's voice that Collin turned to look.

A bright flush enveloped the speaker's cheeks. His eyes gleamed with an emotion Collin recognized—longing.

Paul had seen it, too. He winked at Collin and slipped to the man's side. They moved off. In a little while Paul was back. "Another Englishman has the New Testament in his hands," he whispered.

Collin smiled, but he did not smile later when several men were herded toward the unlit fire. These were the ones who had been caught selling Tyndale's New Testament. Rather than suffer death by fire, they were willing to throw the books into the flames in front of all the spectators.

A gasp arose from the crowd. They pressed closer and craned their necks. Collin saw why. Cardinal Wolsey, the man whose name Collin had learned to dread, was arriving. He was dressed in scarlet from head to foot, even to his gloves. His shoes were embroidered with gold and silver, and inlaid with pearls and precious stones. At a respectful distance, thirty-six bishops, abbots, and priors followed him.

Officials brought in huge baskets of Tyndale's New Testaments and stacked them by the unlit fire. One of Wolsey's men stepped forward and addressed the crowd. "Today we have the pleasure of burning the heretical works of William Tyndale, a traitor to God and his country, who has perverted the sacred Scriptures by putting them in the common tongue and sending them into this kingdom by perfidious followers."

Collin and Paul exchanged glances, Paul, as usual, with a hint of mischief in his dark eyes.

The speaker went on. "The translation and reading

133

of the Bible in the common tongue is heresy. No fire—nay, more than fire—no holocaust will be more pleasing to Almighty God than the one we shall see today when the heretical books of William Tyndale shall be burned."

Cardinal Wolsey signaled for the fire to be lit. Solemn beadles of the church, each holding high a metal-tipped staff, led the five heretics three times around the fire. Each prisoner threw in his fagot and then a copy of the New Testament.

A group of fanatics near Collin began to clap their hands and dance in a ring. When the flames reached their height, the group cheered and babbled to each other. The crackling of the huge blaze silenced them after a few moments, and they moved off. A woman near Collin sobbed aloud. Others tried to quiet her.

"Why do you cry? It is God's will that the works of heresy shall burn. Do you doubt God's will?"

"But why does God want His Word to be kept from His people?" the woman asked.

There were murmurs of assent. Someone exclaimed and drew the attention of the others to the scaffold. This time a priest knelt on the platform. Another priest approached with a knife and scraped the back of the priest's hands until blood showed.

Collin shrank back at the sight. "Why are they doing that, Paul?"

A man nearby answered. "He read a copy of the English New Testament, and now they are defrocking him."

Collin did not need to ask what "defrocking" meant. It was plain. Officers stripped the priest of his clerical vestments until at last he stood in the simple tunic of a layman.

The officials led the ex-priest away.

"What will happen now?" Collin asked.

"He'll be punished."

Collin grabbed Paul's arm. "But if even people within the church want the Scriptures in English, there'll be no stopping it now, will there?"

Paul grinned. "That's what I've been saying all the time. Go back to Worms and tell Sir William to keep up his smuggling. We'll do our part at this end."

Collin decided to do what Paul said.

∘　∘　∘

A few weeks later, Collin reached Worms. For an afternoon he told William Tyndale every detail he could remember about the distribution of the New Testaments. Tyndale listened with flushed cheeks, sometimes chuckling, sometimes frowning, sometimes rubbing his hands with satisfaction. At last he stood up, stretched, and sighed. "I must set to work."

For the first time Collin noticed Roye's belongings were gone. "Where is Roye?" he asked.

Tyndale sighed again. "Roye took his back wages and I haven't seen him since. I bade him farewell for our two lives and a day longer."

Collin reflected on the rascally ex-monk, who in spite of his love of money and gossip, had been of real help to Tyndale.

William Tyndale sighed for the third time. "There is so much comparison necessary in translating. I do need help." He looked at Collin. "Would you like to be my assistant? I dare not trust anyone else."

In the first heart-stopping moment, doubts crowded Collin's mind: He was too young—he didn't know enough about languages—he might be a hindrance instead of a help. Then he felt a Presence within himself, like the one he had witnessed at Little Sodbury when William Tyndale had first realized his mission to translate the Bible. Now it was as if time had stopped, or rather as if there were no such thing as time. Collin understood and accepted with all his heart his own true mission—to assist William Tyndale in putting God's Word before the English people.

Tyndale was smiling at him. "Do you have any doubts?"

"No, sir, none," Collin answered steadily.

"Very well, then. I must set to work. Are my pens ready?"

Collin checked the study table. "Yes, Sir William."

"Is there enough ink?"

"Yes, sir. Plenty."

"Are there any spies at the door?"

Although William Tyndale sounded amused, Collin took the question seriously. Had anyone followed him? He was sure no one had.

"No, Sir William, not at the moment, anyway."

Tyndale sat down and picked up a pen. "I predict that the church will not burn my work—nor me—until God's will is accomplished." He moved up another chair for Collin, ran his finger down the column of a book, and began to make notes.

In a moment he was lost in thought. Collin hesitated. Should he sit down beside Tyndale—or should he tend to other matters first? He fingered the money bag tucked inside his clothes. Thanks to Tyndale's brother and other English merchants, there would be a constant supply. There would be just time to go to the market and buy cheese and fruit for supper. After all, as Tyndale's assistant, Collin would have to see that Tyndale ate. Tyndale would need all his natural strength to fulfill his mission of translating, printing—and smuggling—the next batch of Scriptures into England.

Collin left the room quietly. For the first time he realized how hungry he was. He had forgotten to eat all day, and he knew that William Tyndale had forgotten, too.

## The End

Author's note: in 1536, ten years after the close of our story, William Tyndale died at the stake. His last words were, "Lord, open the King of England's eyes." His prayer was heard. Two years after his death, the English Bible was placed in every parish in England. From then on, the Bible made its triumphant entry into nearly every home. Now, more than four hundred years later, 90 percent of what Tyndale translated is retained in the King James Version of the Bible.

# THE AUTHOR

Louise A. Vernon was born in Coquille, Oregon. Her grandparents crossed the plains in covered wagons as young children.

She earned her BA degree from Willamette University, Salem, Oregon, and studied music at Cincinnati Conservatory. She took advanced studies in music in Los Angeles, after which she turned to Christian journalism. Following three years of special study in creative writing, she began her successful series of religious-heritage juveniles. She teaches creative writing in the San Jose public school district.

Mrs. Vernon re-creates for children the stories of Reformation times and acquaints them with great figures in church history. She has traveled throughout England and Germany researching firsthand the settings for her stories. In each book she places a child on the scene with the historical character and involves him in an exciting plot.

The National Association of Christian Schools, representing more then 8,000 Christian educators, honored *Ink on His Fingers* as one of the two best children's books with a Christian message released in 1972.

Mrs. Vernon is author of *Peter and the Pilgrims* (early America), *Strangers in the Land* (the Huguenots), *The Secret Church* (the Anabaptists), *The Bible Smuggler* (William Tyndale), *Key to the Prison* (George Fox and the Quakers), *Night Preacher* (Menno Simons and the Anabaptists), *The Beggars' Bible* (John Wycliffe), *Ink on His Fingers* (Johann Gutenberg), *Doctor in Rags* (Paracelsus and the Hutterites), *Thunderstorm in Church* (Martin Luther), *A Heart Strangely Warmed* (John Wesley), *The Man Who Laid the Egg* (Erasmus), and *The King's Book* (the King James version of the Bible).